This Too Can Be Yours

also by Beth Lisick:

Monkey Girl

This Too Can Be Yours

Beth Lisick

Manic D Press
San Francisco

For Eli

Thanks and praise to all my collaborator friends, especially Andrew Borger, David Cooper, George Cremaschi and Tara Jepsen. Special thanks to Jan Richman and the amazing one-stop-shoppingness of her friendship.

Published with the assistance of the California Arts Council. "Credit Card Test" originally appeared in slightly different form in *6,500*.

Cover design: Scott Idleman/Blink
Printed in Canada

Library of Congress Cataloging-in-Publication Data

Lisick, Beth, 1968-
   This too can be yours / Beth Lisick.
      p. cm.
   ISBN 0-916397-73-4 (trade pbk. original : alk. paper)
   1. San Francisco (Calif.)--Fiction. 2. Humorous stories, American.
3. Young women--Fiction. I. Title.
   PS3562.I77 T47 2001
   813'.54--dc21

                                        2001005507

Distributed by Publishers Group West

Contents

We Call It Blog

Good morning everybody in cyberspace!!!

I bet you're all wondering how my big date with K____ went.
(She reads this online diary and asked me not to put her name in
here.) I don't know what it is with some people. I've told her how I
get like 13,000 hits a day and that if things work out with us, she
could be a weblebrity too, but she's not buying it. Yet. Mwah-ha-
ha!

So, the date went really, really well. We started off at The
Frog Hut which, for all my non-loyal readers, is the coolest bar
ever. Floor to ceiling with frog paraphernalia. Ceramic frog figu-
rines, macrame frogs, rubber and glass frogs and even a huge chan-
delier covered in frog Shrinky-Dinks. The owner is this whacked-
out old lady who always wears green and says, "Ribbit!" instead of

hello, goodbye and thank you. Kind of like the use of the word Aloha in Hawaii, where you will remember I spent a week with <u>my family</u> last year. K____ has been a big fan of my work for some time now, so she had a lot of questions for me. It was like being on a talk show where I got to be the guest for the whole hour!

Hold on. I see the messenger with the pastries coming up the stairs. Okay, I'm back. There's some big meeting going on for the whole company, so once they're all tucked in the conference room with their cinnabuns, I'll have at least an hour of peace. God, the pastry girl was actually kind of cute in that post-slacker way. It was like I could picture her in faded corduroys and a <u>Kneeling Troll</u> shirt even though she was wearing khakis and an apron. That's the good thing about working front reception for these jerks. Cute girls are constantly coming in for one thing or another. Anyway, back to the date....

So, get this. We have a couple beers and we're not fully flirting yet (though I did brush my left hand against her forearm on accident, which I gathered she noticed but did not mention anything about) and it turns out that she's bought every single one of <u>my comics</u> and even downloaded the <u>videos</u> I put up of my readings! I had no idea when she asked me out that she even knew that I was Timothy Lotkiss. Even though a lot of people know my name and what I do, I can still walk around generally undisturbed by the unwashed masses. LOL. We met in person at <u>Sudsy's party</u> last Saturday. I didn't notice her at first, but then she came up and started talking about *The Hobbit* and it was like, Where did this chick come from? My fantasies? She was into the whole Middle Earth geek thing in a totally ironic way, too. Cool!!

Turns out she had even found that <u>hidden link</u> I put up last month - and you know what that means. She must have completed all four levels of <u>Timothy Trivia</u> to get to it. There we are having our first date and she already knows at what age I lost my virginity, my childhood babysitter's name AND my favorite bar. (Frog Hut. Duh!) I was blown away knowing she'd seen all nine hours of footage of me sleeping, and then it dawned on me, "Whoa. This girl has already seen the inside of my bedroom and she still wants to go out with me." Things were going well indeed.

We decide to head over to Redi-Room, this divey place that you might remember from my wild night with Sabine (Hi Sabine! How are things back home in Salzburg? I still have your friend's checkbook. Is she mad at me? Email me her address and I will send it right away!) K___ suggests we play pool because she knows I am a total pool addict and guess what? She already has an entire roll of quarters because she remembered the drunken rant I wrote about how I can never part with my own quarters because they're so valuable for laundry, parking meters, video booths, etc. I end up winning all six games and I can't help but wonder if she's letting me win because of all that crap that went down with Linda (punk rock goddess!) on New Year's Eve. (New pics just posted!)

Oh my god. Ray from LaughPlanet just called and they want me to make an appearance at some show tonight. Even though I planned to just hole up with my bong and work on my novel all night, I agreed. I figure if I just keep plugging away, keeping a high profile and all that, one of these days I'll strike the jackpot. It's just a matter of time before there's a producer or an agent or a relative of one of these types in the audience. Ray says there'll be plenty of free beer tonight, too. It's so weird how I can have thousands of fans from all over the world who know and love my work, yet I can barely afford to get by in this city. At least I'm in good company with a lot of other starving artists. Shout out to Charles, John, Lester, etc. You guys rip!

Let me get serious for a second here. It just really freaks me out to know that I am as talented as any of those motherfuckers who are famous and I am still faxing lunch menus for sys admin's wearing relaxed-fit slacks. But you know what? I'm only 28 and just starting to do my best work right now. I am presently hitting my stride. Plus, I still have all my hair unlike that poseur Kiddo Larsen who thinks he's God's gift to po-mo satire. Did you hear him on National Fix last week? That tired riff he did on gated communities? I debuted my whole <u>ode to America's changing suburban landscape</u> at least two years ago.

Back to K____. I think I am in love. I truly do. I have met a lot of my readers and fans over the years and there's always the potential when I meet a girl who knows and loves my work that something's going to happen. It's like we get the whole "getting to know you" thing out of the way because she already knows almost everything about me from <u>my archives</u> and doing a <u>web search of my name</u>. Some couples probably spend years playing catch up with their histories, but with me, we can hit the ground running. I feel so lucky. We're able to talk about <u>my new ideas</u> and <u>my new projects</u> right away. We can talk about the future. And did I mention she has the bar code to my first graphic novel tattooed on her shoulder?

Who's a star? I'm a star.

Whoops. Meeting's over! Time to suck up to The Man.

Best Of

My crying had turned into hiccuping and soon enough the barf started flowing. This was when I knew it was time to look into yoga or stop eating cheese for awhile. Something to make me feel more healthy that wasn't quitting drinking. Meditation or cutting out pills for the month of March maybe. I may have been squatting in an oleander wearing a poorly manufactured halter top while everyone else was up there at the party drinking mojitos and doing their little talent show or whatever, but at least I was alone.

And fucking Kendall. "Tits aflame!" she kept saying on the way over. She was so sure she was going to win first prize by trotting out that trick she does with her nipples. Lighting them on fire. Honk shoo. She was so into her tits. 33 years old, a couple years younger than me, but still. It's not Spring Break anymore, is it?

Plus, fire tricks? What is it, 1993 or something? Fire tricks and those fucking fighting robots. And '80s-themed rollerskating parties. And that *Gong Show* shit. I am exhausted by the thought of another fake prom party with corsages and Polaroids. I felt like the flame on a long, tall fireplace match someone was constantly trying to extinguish with a laborious waft of bad breath. Barely flickering and put upon.

At first, I was having a good enough time at the party. I didn't know too many people, just my brother and Kendall, but there was a big wheel of brie wrapped in phyllo and an open bar. The hosts, this total golden couple, who probably knew how to sail and cure olives in their clawfoot bathtub, owned the multimedia p.r. company Kendall was temping for. Their gigantic Edwardian had just been completely redone to maintain its ye olde charm, but with earthquake retrofitting, modern plumbing, and an industrial restaurant-style kitchen. Rich people with bad taste are one thing: fuckers. But rich people with good taste? Forget it. They just make me want to slit my throat from ear to ear.

I hadn't planned anything for the talent show so I thought maybe I'd do an improvised dance routine. Maybe break into my *Flashdance* "Maniac" shuffle that everyone loves so much. It was sort of my calling card. My brother had just performed and everyone was going nuts. Strangers. Strangers love my brother. His talent was playing Quiet Riot's "Cum On Feel the Noize" on the musical saw. He's such a dick, so clever. He goes by our last name: Keegan. His name's actually Stu, but he makes everybody call him Keegan with sort of a pathetic vengeance. "Nice to meet you," he says, and then after a slight pause, "Keegan!" When old friends slip up, he busts in with a prompt correction. No, really, I feel like saying. That is your name. Let people call you that. Are you too special to be a Stuart? Must you jump aboard the reinvention bandwagon? Keegan. A perfect soap opera name for someone starring in his own little soap opera.

I started talking to some guy who owned a web design company. You should also know that sometimes when I laugh really hard, I start crying. Not just crying, but sobbing, not like most people who get watery eyes and brag, "I laughed so hard I cried!" If I'm laughing at a joke... well, I guess no one really laughs at jokes. I haven't laughed at a joke since "How do you know when it's bedtime at Michael Jackson's house?" but say I'm laughing and I've had too much to drink or haven't been sleeping well or I flash on all the lonely people in the world with big hearts and no love to share, I just lose it. Uncontrollable, shoulder-shrugging sobs.

The guy, Ted, and I had been chatting about how he'd spent New Year's in Cuba, everyone was going to Cuba. Then he made a comment about my top, which happens every time I wear it. It's one of those halters made by some old school Harley-mama-turned-straight and they're flying off the rack at the store where I work. We buy them for ten bucks a pop and sell them for sixty, but I get a discount because I'm the assistant manager. It's a piece of material the size of a hankie with pieces of crap sewn on by hand. Foreign coins. Exotic matchbooks. Action figures. Mine happened to have old concert ticket stubs from The Fillmore. I mean, you can't even wash this shit and most drycleaners won't take them because they get messed up in the machines. The halters had recently got written up in the weekly newspaper as Best Something or Other. In case you haven't noticed, every square inch of this city has been awarded Best Something or Other at this point. I swear I saw a Coke machine near General Hospital that would sell you a can for fifty cents and the next week there it was in the paper as Best Homage to Refrigerator Perry. Nothing undiscovered and nowhere to hide.

So after the guy fondles one of my stubs, The Cure or Siouxsie and The Banshees, he tells me the name of his company. "PrancingGazelle.com," he says. "Elegant web design for surfisticates of all stripes." And he says it like that. The tag line. I just started laughing because it was so classic. (Animal names were particularly popular at the time - everybody loves an animal! - plus fruits, vegetables and outer space themes were also big.) At first he's being polite when I start in, but I'm telling you, I couldn't stop. I was laughing about how he'd delivered it, like maybe I was a potential surfisticate that could use some elegant web design. Then came the name itself. Not just his company, but everybody's. It weirded me out hearing people say, "Well, now that Yahoo! is searching with Google..." or "No. I left Leap Frog and I'm over at Dotcomix now," or "We made an executive decision to go with Holy Guacamole Interactive over Kit and Kaboodle Technologies." I just started speaking gibberish because I thought he'd understand.

"Really, Ted?" I said as the tears were starting to squirt. "Well, have you ever visited BlingBling or slorfed inside a Grabasket? I generally check my mail with Dudeballs because I have a Greenbelly connection through JumpingOtter who've just been bought by Scagwhistle.com." I was going so hard at the end, I think I might have knocked over a drink. Someone knocked over a drink because I heard a crash and everyone went "Woo!" like they do when they mean "This partay is getting off the ground!" Kendall ran over just as the guy was slowly backing away, keeping his eyes on me, nodding and biting his lower lip like a man does on a sitcom when he's trying to get rid of the weird neighbor.

I was going full tilt boogie with the crying now because it was so fucking funny. I couldn't control myself to get the words out and explain, so I guess everybody thought I had just heard some horrible news. The hostess came out from somewhere with a tray of champagne.

"What the hell? Who is that?" Her halter was covered in mousetraps.

Little strings of saliva were connecting my lower lip to my

top lip whenever I opened my mouth and pretty soon I was inadvertently blowing those little spit bubbles. Kendall knew. Why didn't she start laughing like she always did? She looked all worried. I heard a fire engine going down the street and I saw her hand over her mouth and all of a sudden I thought for a second that she had called an ambulance on me.

"Come with me. Come with me." She was grabbing me by the arm and pulling me towards the bathroom. Her fingers made my skin all prickly. I just had to explain to her and the group that was crowding around how funny it was. "No! No!" I kept shouting, "Just listen to me! SHUT UP SHUT UP SHUT UP." My face was all red and I was squeezing my eyes closed into little raisins. I was only yelling so they would pay attention. As soon as I calmed down, I could explain it better. And they would all laugh, too.

"Sadie! Sadie!" she kept saying once we were inside the bathroom. The music got quieter. "You have to stop!"

My nose was dripping with snot and my chest was heaving. "But, you know! You know! The Prancing, The Prancing," I was getting choked up. "Ga-ga-gazelle!" I lost it again. Laughing and crying.

"What are you talking about? What is wrong with you?" The crease in her forehead was like a riverbed. She started stage-whispering, "You know what? You are like, being psycho. You are Gena Rowlands in *Woman Under the Influence*."

That was one of my favorite movies and she knew it! "Pffft! Pffft!" I do a killer imitation of when Gena's character makes those farting sounds and is waving away invisible flies in the air. I had it down. I wanted everyone to see. There might be a few Cassavetes fans around who would appreciate it. Then they'd know I was funny and not really crying and weird. I ran out of the bathroom. "Pfft! Pffft!" I was going. "Pfft! Pffft!" Swatting flies.

Stuart grabbed me (where had he been?) ripping one of my

concert tickets, and I flipped out. "Stuart Pooart! Stuart Pooart!" It's what I called him when we were kids and he hated it. It was probably especially embarrassing for him because he'd introduced himself as Keegan to everyone at the party. Who was Stuart? Not him, obviously.

Then I remember flying up in the air and hitting the floor hard. It got super quiet. Stuart was walking away rubbing his knuckles and where were my shoes? I hadn't gotten a pedicure all winter and my toes looked awful. I know it sounds stupid, but that's when I started crying for real. I was in the mush pot. My lower jaw felt crooked and when I looked up at Kendall and wiped some blood from my nose, she looked so serious. Whispering to people I'd never met and that's when I went for the front door. Crawling at first until I smacked into an amplifier with my forehead and then I stood up and bolted.

I expected someone to come after me. I didn't go far at first. Just around the side of the house so they could find me, and threw up a few times in the bushes. I tried to listen to see if they were talking about me, but the music was too loud. A lady was doing karaoke Patsy Cline. I am so over people doing Patsy at karaoke. They are ruining her!

It got super cold, but I wouldn't go back. No way. If those idiots didn't know what was so funny, fine. They could just picture me booking down the middle of Divisadero with snot pouring down my face, barf in my hair, barefoot. Dried blood and red wine crusting in the corners of my mouth. I moved out of the bushes and started running.

Bad News Bridesmaid

The nerve of some people, the flipping nerve. There I was lying awake, all sweaty under the covers with my flame-retardant nightgown so far twisted around my body it was practically lapping itself, and I'm sure Sandy was floating on Cloud 9. Doing the Macarena on the Lido deck. Or better yet, learning a whole new dance I haven't even heard of yet, a dance craze that would soon sweep the nation and she learned it first as a newlywed on board that Skylark Samba Honeymoon Cruise. Thinking about it made my feet itch. I threw the pillow over my face, having forgotten I'd just smeared it with Preparation H to reduce bloat (beauty secret of the Hollywood stars) and she was probably taking a moonlit stroll after feasting at a buffet and taking in a magic show. Holding hands under the captain's bridge. Cracking jokes with the purser. Fending off advances from the ship's horny doctor.

I was so delirious from tossing and turning I started to feel like I had actually been on a number of cruises myself sometime during the late '70s to mid '80s. Had I? I could picture it perfectly. Loads of shuffleboard and daiquiris. Giddy with laughter, a pinata tossed over my shoulder after daytripping in Ensenada. I think I even had a couple no-strings affairs with minor celebrities who were waiting for their pilots to get picked up. Now that was fun. The good old carefree days when love was exciting and new. They were expecting me. And now where am I? All bundled up in the dark like a seething newborn opossum. I needed to compose the letter in my head so come morning, I could dash it off and there it would be, ticking away like a timebomb for her return.

Dear Sandy,

You know how much I love you and how excited I am that you finally got married. I mean, how many people are lucky enough to find a partner who's an investment banker, metal sculptor, community activist, interior decorator, auto mechanic and certified EMT?

Whew! I've got to catch my breath!

You know you are my best friend, you always will be, and I'm so honored you chose me to play such a crucial role in your ceremony. I know it's because you also love and respect me, so bearing that in mind - the love and respect I know you have for me - there's just one little thing, a tiny thing (even tinier than the rock on that ring he gave you ... just kidding! You know I've always appreciated that you weren't showy or ostentatious and I guess neither is he) but I just wondered...

Why did you select that particular dress for me to wear?

It's okay that it cost $250. Love has no price tag. We all know that. And the fact that I had to take off work to get it fitted and pick it up during my lunch hour, getting a parking ticket in the process, well, talk about added value! It jacks it up to well over $300.

I am now the owner of a $300 dress. Who'd have thought I'd ever buy one of those? That I didn't even care for.

I mean, I know you suggested getting it altered again later, to make a nice knee-length cocktail dress that would be appropriate for, what, I don't know. You tell me. Plus, I don't think I've ever worn that color before and Sandy, honest Injun, I don't think you've ever worn that color before. They invented that color during the fourth season of *Dynasty* and it should have been cancelled for poor ratings, if you know what I mean.

The dyed-to-match shoes were a whole other thing. Thought you should know that all day long I had a severe case of toe cleavage and by the end of the day my feet smelled like the cream filling in a Twinkie that'd been smeared along the rim of a diaper pail. I am sorry. That was gross. But true!

I know I'm getting a little carried away here, but do you think, in the deepest part of your imagination, that same imagination that allowed you to try to put a shoehorn up my butt when we were little girls, that you wanted everyone else, the other women, the bridesmaids, your friends, to look so horrible so it would make you look that much better?

I know that sounds terrible, but then again I also know you wanted to grow your perm out and tone up your flapping triceps before the big day. And you didn't do that now, did you?

Don't get me wrong. You know you were a stunning bride. Your dress, a hand-tailored copy of your grandmother's gown from the '20s. Beautiful. Our gowns, on the other hand, were from a bridal store in that giant designer outlet mall near Gilroy.

Oh, I know you went the extra mile and hired a professional to do our makeup and give us elaborate hairdos. A different professional than the one who gave you your look for the day.

So while you looked sleek and retro, like Louise Brooks in *Pandora's Box*, I looked like a fucking Judd over there. And not Ashley. You know I meant the other two. The singing ones. You, standing in the shade underneath the willow tree for the duration of the hour-long ceremony, and me, mysteriously placed in direct sunlight, sweating like a hog.

I mean, it was your day. You were in charge. And it was educational to see what your idea of a classy party is. But there's one last thing... Face it. There was one handsome, available groomsman, the sort of Latin-looking soccer player one. Uh-huh, Angelo, with the earring. And he is not gay! That guy with the Guatemalan fanny pack was his roommate. You paired him up with your sister. Hello! Your sister is married, even if she was doing body shots with the teenage videographer behind the toolshed. I am single and you stuck me with Jim's college roommate, Stuart Keegan. The man is shaped like a pear and when he got drunk and took off his shirt his belly button was the size of my fist. My fist!

He followed me around all night long and shoved me toward the bouquet when I didn't even want it. I didn't want the bouquet, Sandy. He pushed me right towards it and that's why I elbowed your cousin with the cleft palate. As soon as I came home I tossed it over the fence into my neighbor's steaming compost pile.

I just thought I'd bring these things up because I was worried you had some sort of problem with me and that's why you treated me so poorly on your special day.

Welcome home,
Marie

P.S. I know you are passive-aggressive so I have just resolved to take all this with a grain of salt if that's what you want.

I Got The Beat

If I were a magician or a prostitute, a story about performing for a private party would make a lot more sense. Unfortunately, I was hired to read poetry.

This must be the brainchild of someone who has never actually attended a poetry reading, I thought to myself as I listened over the phone. Why else would someone consider this remotely appropriate for entertainment purposes? Her answer spoke volumes.

"We're a young technology company called Holy Guacamole Interactive and we thought it would be, you know, fun for the launch of our new product!"

I paused for a moment, letting us both savor the unchecked esprit of her reply.

"And how much could you pay me?" I hedged, knowing full

well that people all over this city were spending ridiculous amounts of money on making their companies seem cool. "It's sort of short notice."

"The party budget say $200," she replied. "And you only have to read for ten minutes."

As soon as I hung up the phone, I fired off an email to my parents.

> Dear Mom and Dad,
> Hope you had a nice time at the dog show in Milwaukee and met some interesting Portuguese Water Dog lovers from around the country. Things here are looking up. I am now commanding one thousand two hundred dollars an hour for my spoken word appearances.

The gig was at one of those small boutique hotels downtown. You know the kind always featured in *Vanity Fair* for doing kooky things like stocking the room with tons of junk food because it is so irreverent and wild to look at a green Hostess Snoball nestled up next to a split of champers in the sleek chrome mini-fridge.

I walk in through the front door and as I approach the concierge, she starts doing her job. Pausing a moment to silently judge me.

"Go to the third floor," she says, regarding me like a cheap Holiday Inn washcloth that's just been used to wipe up a dripping vagina. "Ask for Lucas. He's the party planner."

I step off the elevator and am immediately accosted by a compact man with a gorgeous head of hair that's been wrapped into a neat bun with a tropical hair scrunchie.

"Oh, my god," he says. "Puh-leeze tell me you're the talent. We've got to get you changed immediately! You can put on your costume in room 314."

It sounded remarkably like he was serious.

"Costume?" I say. "Nobody said anything to me about a costume. Is this a costume party?"

This is when I realize that I am the multimedia version of a birthday party clown.

Lucas turns on his heel and heads down the hall shouting "Marnie! Marnie! The poetess is here and she says nobody told her about the costume!"

I follow after him becoming increasingly alarmed at the sight of professionals dressed in "biz casz" milling about with cosmopolitans. Then I get a load of what Lucas has done with an ordinary hotel conference room. Oh, Lucas! You didn't!

He has turned the place into a mini tiki lounge. The industrial carpeting is covered with straw mats, Polynesian fabrics are draped from the ceiling, and the walls are lined with bamboo. The only light emanates from a couple of laptops and some of those Pier 1 Imports tiki torches that really hit their stride in the summer of '92. Sure I needed the money, but how was I going to get though this?

Momentarily channeling the Bionic Woman, my head begins to rotate ever so slightly to the left as my keen sense of hearing picks up the signals of ice in a cocktail shaker. Like Patty Duke playing Helen Keller at the water pump, I move towards it in the darkness. It is then that I make the decision that I should turn, once again, to the sweet, sweet liquor that dulls the pain.

The bartender is chatty. He wants to know what I do for the company, what I think of the new product and how much my stock options are worth. I tell him the truth.

"This is sort of weird," I say, "but I'm here to read poetry."

"No way!" he says. "You're the beat poet? I heard about this. That is so cool!" I start explaining, but he slides me a, what else, cosmo, and keeps talking. "I totally thought you'd be older. Wow! I read *On The Road*, like, three times or twice at least."

I'm on my second free cosmo when Lucas comes bustling in shouting, "There you are! Listen, we've got to get you ready. William, the big guy, the CEO, can't wait to meet you."

We step out into the hall and this enormous man who looks sort of like a cross between John Tesh and a bigger, doofier version of John Tesh, is standing outside one of the rooms, walking backwards and beckoning me in.

"So, you're her!" he says. "The beat poet! It's very nice to meet you, MAN."

"I'm not really a beat poet," I say.

He tells me to sit down while broadly gesturing to the only furniture in the room. A gigantic bed.

"Do you think it's going to be too dark in there for you?" William asks. "To read the poems?"

I tell him it doesn't really matter because I have some stuff memorized. The darker the better as far as I was concerned.

William is taken aback. "Oh, no," he says. "There must be a misunderstanding. No, no, no," he says again, working overtime to eke out a chuckle. "I've got the poems right here."

A white hot panic surges through my body.

Lucas charges in, "We've found a beret!" My head snaps to the right. "Well, it's not exactly black, is it?" Lucas says. "But we're in a pinch! It'll have to do."

"Can I go get another drink?" I ask.

"No! Not right now!" John Teshish says. "I want to make sure you can pronounce all the words in my poems."

"You wrote the poems?" I am stunned.

"Yes, I did," he beams.

Like a sullen teenager, I grab the pages from him. They are all rhyming poems about the new product. I remind myself again that no one will ever find out about this.

"Yep. No problem," I say. "I'll just go in and get a drink and go over it a couple times in my head."

I start for the door and he stands up, blocking it. "Wait! I want to make sure you know HOW to read it."

Usually, I don't give a shit if people say stuff like this to me. I don't expect anyone to look at me and somehow know that I have mastered the basic rules of phonetics or that I have experience speaking in public, but I give him a look that feels exactly like a look I would have given my mom when I was thirteen. It's a look that says, "I am so sure!"

He doesn't notice. He is on a roll. He has now launched his hands into that position where you pretend you're a movie director lining up your shot. Big old thumbs sticking out like Ball Park franks.

"Did you see that, what was it called?" he says. That Mike Meyers movie? Where he was the, uh, you know, the I Got Married To... No, wait. Married to the... No, uh..."

"*So I Married an Ax Murderer?*" I offer.

"Yes!" he says. "Did you see it?"

"No," I say.

"And you call yourself a beat poet?"

I just laugh. I laugh and laugh. Something in my laugh, something that is saying, Please, Please Let Me Out Of Here, makes him rethink the whole false imprisonment thing. He steps aside.

Back at the party, a lady with a laptop asks me if I want to see the product demo.

"Oh, no thanks!" I say. I was nice.

"Okay, whatever!" she says. "If you don't want your life changed, fine!"

Lucas approaches me with the beret. "You forgot your beret," he says. "Remember to give it back to that lady over there in the red sweater after you're finished."

I stare into middle distance nodding.

"Right there!" he says again. I look across the room and a woman smiles and waves. She looks proud that her hat will be part of the show.

After another cocktail, Lucas gives me the thumbs up. As I move to the front of the room, I let the beret casually slip from my fingers onto the woven mats.

At this point, I am drunk, addled, a little fuzzy about what my role is here. While logically I realize that they have hired me to show up and read from a piece of paper, I am somehow interpreting this moment as a platform to slur out a pathetic half-baked diatribe about being a writer and not having any money and whoring yourself in the weirdest ways because maybe it'll make good material, and hey, isn't this strange for you guys, too?

As I continue rambling, I watch the expressions in the room change from curious anticipation to Who Took A Shit in My Cargo Pants??

Determined to give the most over-the-top faux beatnik recitation I possibly can, I launch into the "poems" and complete my act with sarcastic finger snapping. Dig!

The crowd roars. It's possibly the best reception I have ever gotten for a performance. As I move through the crowd, people shower me with backslaps and compliments and business cards. I grab my check from Lucas. He doesn't mention the beret, so I don't either.

Grit in the Oil

It's not even like I needed the money that bad or anything. With this guy, it was just that he was my friend Steven's friend. I'd done some stuff for Steven about a year ago when he was worried about his wife. His ex-wife now. Just a little video work was all, but then he asked me to do a favor for his friend, like he sometimes does, and I couldn't really say no. I didn't want to say no. I realize I should probably stop doing this sneaking-for-hire shit at some point, but it's addictive. It's better than porn or drugs and in the end, I make money as opposed to blowing it.

"She's a fucking babe," this friend of Steve's told me. "She's fucking hot."

We were at the bar having a beer. I was technically supposed to be on duty with the limo but business was slow so we were sorting the deal out over some drinks.

I asked him how I would know which girl she was. And how do we know she'll get in my limo if she didn't call for one?

"You'll know her because she's fucking hot," the friend said.

He handed me a picture. It was from one of those photo booths. Black and white and pretty washed out. He didn't have the whole strip of them, though. Just one little square.

I looked at it close. The girl was putting on a really sexy face, the tip of her tongue touching the bottom part of her top lip. She was pretty, but just regular pretty. Big eyes. There was no way I could recognize her from this. I handed it back to the guy.

"Didn't I say she was hot? Right? Wait until you see her in person." He took a swig from his beer and made a big "Ah!" sound while checking himself out in the mirror behind the bar.

Steven helped me out, saying, "I just don't think he's going to be able to find her with that to go on, Dean."

I said maybe I should hold up one of those signs at the gate when she gets off the plane. With her name on it.

"Dude's a fucking genius," Dean says to Steven. To me he says, "Dude, you're a fucking genius! She'll think somebody called it to impress her. That kind of shit is always happening to her. Industry assholes are always trying to get in her pants."

I guess I looked surprised because the guy goes, "Because she's so hot, that's why!" Then he leans into my shoulder and says, "She's going to get my band signed."

"Oh, cool," I said. I looked at Steven. Where does he find these guys?

"And, and," he's tapping me on the shoulder, "and I've been fucking her."

I nod my head like we're doing serious business, and say, "Gotcha."

I wasn't about to give that guy my phone number, so the next morning I get a call from Steven saying everything is still on. He gave me the flight info and all I had to do was stand at the gate with the sign, get her into the limo and record our conversation as I drove her to the hotel. It seemed pretty stupid, but whatever. He said Dean told him he wanted to find out what other local bands she was checking out while she was here, but he thought there was something else, too. He thought it had something to do with finding out who else she was sleeping with.

Man, I wish he didn't tell me that. I just kept thinking about that guy's ham hands wrapped around his sweaty beer and how his breathing got all weird and uneven when he talked about her. On some jobs, more information is definitely better than too little, but not this type of thing. And for only two hundred bucks? My stomach went a little sour. Three years ago I was working in the public library and going to church and now I was aiding and abetting stalkers. Don't get me wrong. I hated working in that library and my renewed interest in Jesus was only for my girlfriend at the time, but still. Sometimes I feel like I was born wearing a coat of porcelain that just keeps gradually chipping away. Now I've got all these rusty spots peeking out and the only way I'll ever be right again is to get completely sandblasted and start from scratch.

Getting my car everyday is always sort of an ordeal. There's this moblike ring of limo companies up in Twin Peaks and it always feels shady pulling up to the apartment complex they run the business out of. Merdad is my man, except he recently told me to start calling him Mike because he thinks Merdad sounds too much like Spanish for shit. My gate fee is $70 for an eight-hour shift, so I pay Mike the money and get rolling. He stands there with his big fat fingers smoking one of those skinny ladies' cigarettes, a Capri or something, and I take off down the hill. Before I hit the freeway, I stop at my favorite corner store for batteries for the tape recorder and the owner tries to sell me a rubberband ball again. I can't believe him. He and his brother got into the Guinness Book for having the biggest rubberband ball in the world and now they're trying to capitalize on it by selling autographed replicas for ten bucks. Would you pay ten dollars for a rubberband ball about the size of a tennis ball just because it was made and signed by the man who owns the largest rubberband ball in the world? Well, today I did. Today I broke down and bought one.

They keep the Guinness record holder in the back of the store covered by a faded Mighty Mouse bedsheet, but today, right when I'm buying the batteries, he's unveiling it and rolling it out into the aisle for some people. They might have been his relatives, I'm not sure. Everyone is all dressed up like they'd just been to church and they seemed so proud of the guy and his ball. They all kept patting it, giving it little slaps and punches. When I put my batteries down on the counter and he said as he always does, "Hey, friend. How about a lucky baby ball? His mother is very famous!" I agreed. The family claps and makes universal noises of elation as I open my wallet.

Traffic to the airport isn't bad at all. I start thinking about how when I was a kid I loved tape-recording people. I got this big clunky recorder for my birthday one year, I was probably about eight, and I was relentless. I used to make radio shows with these girls down the block, but every time they weren't looking, I'd press the record button. I loved catching people off guard by playing back to them something they just had said a minute ago. When I could tell my parents were about to go to bed, I'd run into their room and hide it under their bed. I had these fantasies about hearing them say secret adult stuff or else catching them talking about me, but usually all I could hear was the t.v. The last time I ever did it, I listened to the tape in the morning before I went down for breakfast and my parents' voices were coming in loud and clear. My mom kept saying, "When are we going to tell him? How are we going to get through this?" She was crying. My dad was trying to comfort her and finally he started sobbing, saying, "He's an alien. Our son is an alien."

I totally fell for it. My head got all hot and I was just kneeling on the carpet, dumbfounded. How could I go down and eat my cereal? Did I have to go to school anymore? Did that mean they weren't really my parents? I don't know what I would have done if the two of them hadn't immediately burst into my room laughing. Just the whole emotional rollercoaster of first thinking I'd caught them in a private conversation, and then realizing they were talking about me, to that very brief moment when I believed I just might be an alien, and then finally, they come storming into my room, laughing their asses off at me. Thinking about this makes me miss my turnoff and I have to get off on the next exit and loop around.

It's not until I'm halfway through the airport, running down a People Mover, that I realize I've forgotten the sign with the girl's name on it out in the car. It's so sad because the original had looked really pro with nice block letters spelled out with a Sharpie, and now I was running really late. When I get to the gate, I borrow a pen from the ticket agent but she says she doesn't have any paper. She is a total liar. I decide not to return the pen, which looks like it was pilfered from a Seattle-area Olive Garden anyway, and I root around in the garbage for something to write on. Newspapers, greasy fast food bags, a diaper. The only thing clean and usable is a huge styrofoam cup. Thank God everyone drinks these jumbo beverages. I write her first name vertically and then I completely space out on her last name. What is it? It's something like Farrar or Ferrara. Ferrero? Fuck. I decide to write Ferrari so I can pretend I did it as a joke. A play on her real name. Mia Ferrari.

I get all ready for everybody to start coming out, trying to picture the girl I saw in the photo, while also making sure my styrofoam cup is attractively displayed. She's the first one off the plane. I bet I could have spotted her even if I'd never seen a picture. Blond, tiny, one of those short, petite people who have the unsettling demeanor of being very much in charge. Talking on her cell phone, wearing tight jeans and a little black top with the word "Superstar" printed out in metal studs. I don't get those shirts at all. Spoiled. Angel. Brat. Princess. I see them a lot when I'm driving around the tourist areas and I can't figure out what they're supposed to make me think. Mostly I just think the girl wearing it is some kind of cockteasing bitch, but maybe that's being too harsh.

She's on her phone, so I step right in front of her and pretend to take a drink from the cup. She looks up at me and I guess I was a little startled cause I accidentally start sucking on the straw. It tastes like banana smoothie. She taps the cup with her cell phone antenna and says, "Cute." Then she hands me her bag and starts walking down the concourse. I follow while she rambles away.

"All right, honey. I'm at the airport now. No, not a cab. I have a driver this time. Probably Paragon Records called for it. I have no idea. The chauffeur wrote my name on a Jamba Juice cup except he spelled it Ferrari, so it's probably Joel. What were you saying when I left? Oh wait, I have another call. Shit. Hello? Oh hi, baby. Yes, I'm here. I'm here now. In San Francisco. How was my flight? Did you just ask me how my flight was? God, that's so embarrassing. What are you going to ask me next? What's my favorite color? Listen, I'm on the other line. I'll call you right back. Ciao. Hi Chuy. So, what's up?"

I skip a little bit to catch up with her, trying to remember what she's saying in case this is something I'm supposed to be catching.

"My flight? What is it with everyone? It's a bus ride in the air,

Chuy. It takes an hour. What do you want to know? I put on my headphones. I don't talk to anyone. I have a drink. I don't eat the peanuts. I wish people would stop making a big deal out of air travel. Like it's a moment, a rite of passage, we all can join hands about and share. Sorry if I'm being a bitch, but if you're going to take this job, you have to know a few things about me. I'm sure Luis told you how touchy I am."

She pulls the phone away from her face and winks at me, then back to the phone, "Hey, is today his last day? Well, give him a big kiss for me. Or don't if you're one of those macho homophobes. I just think people need to stop saying boring things. No offense or anything, but don't you? I mean, how was my flight? Jesus. Okay, let's get my schedule."

She stops cold and leans forward, throwing her hair back in a huge supermodel-like gesture.

"It sounds like you're sucking on an Altoid, honey. Are you? I'm really into the blue ones suddenly. The blue packaging. I don't know why. Hold on... Where am I going?"

She looks back at me and I point to the left. "I'm back. So, I'm staying at The Rex. That's where I stay here. Not The Phoenix, The Rex. In Seattle it's The Camlin, Tucson: it's The Congress. Austin Motel in Austin. The SoHo Grand in New York. You'll learn it all soon. It's a whole strategy thing. It says as much about you as how you take your coffee. Yeah. You know. Black coffee is for ex-junkies and Midwesterners. Sugar only is for people with no sense of style. Cream and sugar is for lightweights, the borderline retarded, and people who don't actually like coffee. Cream only is for indulgent eccentrics. That's cream, by the way, not milk. That's why the tattoo on the small of my back, a rendering of a coffee cup in the artistic style of Communist propaganda posters, has the saying in Japanese kitakana symbols, 'Cream, no sugar.' Why don't you just call me back when you get the schedule together, okay?

Bye!"

She sighs a huge dramatic sigh, looks back at me and smiles. "Sorry about that. You know us L.A. types. Always on the phone."

"Uh, yeah," I say. "Most people I know who have them are always talking on them. They say it's like a, um..." I'm interrupted by her phone ringing.

"Hello? Yes. I think it's sometime tomorrow, but let me call you back." She turns to me and says, "Sorry about that. What did you say?"

"Oh, nothing. Here, we're right here." I open up the door for her and she slides in like she's done it a million times. She stays right by the door, which is good because it's closer to where I put the recorder.

"Wait! Give me that!" She steps out and pulls the suitcase out of my hand.

"Sorry," I say. "I was going to put it in..."

"The trunk?" she snaps. "Well, there's plenty of room for it back here with me."

I slam the door and go around to the front.

"So, do you want to go right to The Rex?" I ask without looking at her.

"How did you know I was staying there?"

"Oh, I heard you on the phone talking. Kind of a bad habit."

"Oh, right. Right. I said it on the phone."

As if on cue, her phone rings again. "Hi. No, I forgot my Palm, that's why we're doing this remember? You can fax the rest to the hotel, but I just have to know a few things. Who am I having cocktails with tonight? Oh my god. Steve's Stony Wetsuit. Is that the stupidest name you've ever heard? Okay. And then dinner is with On Again Off Again, right? God, these band names are so bad. What level is this? Where do I have to take them for dinner? Okay, fine. Just tell me no breakfasts tomorrow. Definitely not rock hours.

I won't do breakfast unless it's after 2 p.m. Tomorrow lunch is Megashimmer? Or is it The Kindling Thieves? How are we supposed to sell bands with names like that? Jesus fuck. I'll call you back." She hangs up the phone and lets out a huge, dramatic sigh.

"Busy day, huh?" I say.

She ignores me and gets on the phone again. "Brent. It's me. I think I'll rent a tacky convertible and drive across the Golden Gate to visit you in the studio tomorrow. Have you guys gone in the hot tub yet? Out on the back porch? I know it's hard. I mean, can't you just imagine Grace Slick with an inch-long splinter wedged in her bare ass after too many vodkas? Hilarious. I'll call you tonight, sweetie. Buh-bye... Did you say something?"

I pretend I think she's still on her phone even though it's clear she's talking to me. She starts dialing.

"Hi. It's me. Did you get my little present? Oh, no! I had it mailed to your work in case what's-her-face freaks out. She's not really your girlfriend, is she? Well, you should have gotten it by now. Hold on, baby. Hello? Chuy! You didn't send that package to my little friend! The soap, the soap! How is he supposed to have been thinking of me while he's touching himself in the shower without the soap? Just forget it. Fuck you. Bye. Sweetie? I'm sorry you didn't get my present, but I guess it doesn't matter because I'm here now. I'm in a limo coming from the airport. Should I swing by and pick you up?"

I see her rolling her eyes in the rearview while she listens. "Okay, whatever. If she has you on a leash, then fine. I'm free for dinner tonight and if you want to see my new underwear, I suggest you make yourself available. Bye!"

She leans up in the seat and starts talking to me. "God, can you believe it? I come all the way from L.A. and it's like I have to force this guy to have sex with me."

I know that's my cue to say something like, "He must be crazy!"

but I only manage a fake laugh.

She sits back again and starts on another phone call. "Hi! It's me—me, Mia—and I'm looking for you, you, you-a! I don't know where you are, but I'm here in S.F. and I really hope you're going to be around the next few days. Call me on my cell."

We're off the freeway, sitting in traffic downtown, when I finally decide to roll up the window between us. She's making me depressed. I can't believe that loser Dean thinks he has some sort of proprietary relationship with this girl. I hope she signs his band and they have a big terrible radio hit. He'll get bloated and disillusioned while doing a 56-city tour to promote it and in the end, the record company will steal all the profits. Then in five years, they'll sell it to Taco Bell and he'll be worse off because he still won't see any money AND he'll be known as the guy with the Taco Bell song. And will I still be the guy helping him stalk women? Yuck. Of course not.

She's on the phone still. She's laying down on the seat kicking her legs in the air. I wonder what it's like to fly all over the country and have people kiss your ass. Worse, it's people who want to be famous kissing your ass.

We're just about up to Market when she starts banging on the glass with her fist screaming, "What the fuck is this? What the fuck?" She's holding up the tape recorder.

What am I supposed to do? It's actually pretty safe up here. The glass is bulletproof so even if Miss Superstar has a gun, she can't touch me.

She's hitting the glass with her palm now and I'm trying not to flinch every time she pounds it. I keep staring straight ahead as the light turns yellow, then red. Fuck. At least I'm not the only car in the middle of the intersection.

She opens the door, tugs her suitcase out and comes around to my window.

"Fucking sleaze!" She's really freaking out. "Who put you up to this? Stuart? Kevin? That bitch at Sony?" She's got the recorder firmly in her palm and proceeds to smash it over and over again on the hood of the limo. People are leaning on their horns anyway and the female half of a homeless couple is cheering her on. "You tell him, sister! You tell that bad man!"

Finally, the light changes and the car in front of me moves. The girl throws the recorder out in the street and it goes skidding along the concrete in a couple pieces. Clicking over to the sidewalk, she turns around one last time to flip me off. This is my most pathetic job yet. And I'm going to have to pay to fix that dent out of my own pocket. When she's almost out of sight, I roll down the window and chuck the rubberband ball at her. I miss. It bounces into the street and a dog runs out to get it.

Old School Ex

"Tricked you, didn't I?" she says, looking right past me and stepping into the apartment. The doorbell rang and I had answered it, something I forgot I wasn't supposed to be doing for awhile for exactly this reason. I was distracted, trying to get the dog to stop chewing the fur off his ass, and the next thing I know, it's like I'm a regular guy who can open his front door. I watch her walk down the long hall into my living room before I follow her.

She's out of breath, pacing. One of the old school exes. Before I got smart.

"It's been awhile," she says.

"Years," I say.

I look back down the hall and see the front door is still open. It's creating a wind tunnel effect, which starts to feel right. I decide not to close it.

"So, what do you want?" I ask.

"That's more like it," she says. "That's how I remember you. So completely bursting with tact."

Trying to avoid one girlfriend disaster and another pops up in her place. They're like Whack-A-Mole. I vow never to answer the door again. Who comes to your door these days anyway? I mean, that you want to see? No one just rings your doorbell and you wind up being happy about it.

I motion toward the couch with a grand sweeping gesture that says All Yours, Baby. She refuses.

"Maybe in a minute," she says. "Maybe after I've gotten some of this out. After I've expunged it from my aching soul maybe I can take a load off," she says.

I watch her scanning the room, looking at my stuff. She goes over to the stereo and lifts up the cover on the turntable to see what I've got on there.

"Excuse me," I say. "Looking for something?"

"I've got an idea," she says. "Why don't you sit? You just might want to be sitting for this."

I sit down on my couch and then think better of it, popping right back up and telling her to get on with it and I don't have all day, okay?

"New piano," she says. She pounds out the *Dragnet* chords. Dah duh-duh-duh.

I lean against the wall. "Listen. Listen," I say, "I don't call you back because we have nothing to say to each other and you know it."

She says, "You know when I saw disaster? You know when I should have run screaming from this thing?"

"You ran screaming a lot of times," I say.

"When you told me you loved me on our second date," she

39

says, examining her nails.

"It's not my fault you didn't believe me," I explain lamely. "That's your problem, isn't it?"

"What?" she says. "And after our second date, I didn't hear from you for a week because you were fucking that Japanese girl you met on tour." Pauses a second for dramatic effect and adds, "Classic." Continuing without missing a beat, she rails on. "I'm really not here two years later to bitch about all the shitty little things that transpired during our shitty little liaison. Indeed," she says, "indeed you proved to be the single worst, most morally deficient human I've ever met. And to this day you still are."

"Thanks," I say icily. "And?"

"I still haven't met someone worse," she says. "Honest. And I've been traveling a lot! I've been places, too, you know," she says. "No, I've moved on. I don't give a rat's ass that you stashed away photos of teenage girls. Young ones. I mean, to your credit, you never asked me to shave my pubic hair and wear tartan schoolgirl skirts. And that was considerate," she says. "I appreciated that so I won't even bring that one up. What's the point really? To talk about your fixation on twelve-year-olds. I'm not even going to mention it.

"I may have gotten drunk and let it slip how you tried to clock me in the face once or twice. Word travels fast and ladies need to be warned, but I'm not even going to bring that up now. I don't want to bring up your anger management problem. That's something else to not talk about," she says.

"So stop talking about it," I say.

"And that thing with the booking agent? Forget it," she says. "There's no reason to go over how humiliating it must have been for you to endlessly lick that tarty L.A. record industry ass because some slut with a Lexus was going to get your band signed. Why would I do that to you? Why would I remind you that all you got in the end was an opening slot for some has-been in Albuquerque and her kicking down your door at the hotel? Woo-hoo," she yells. "ROCK STAR!"

"You know those weren't my photos," I attempt to remind her. "The girls."

"I told you I am over the kiddie porn," she says. "I'm not bringing it up. Why are you bringing it up? No, there are a few other things I need to clear the air about before I get to the meat here. And it doesn't have to do with those other character flaws I won't mention.

"By the way," she sneers, "have you learned to parallel park yet?"

"Shut up," I growl. I'm thinking something about her looks wrong. Her teeth?

She says, "It's not even worth asking why you used to wake up on a Saturday morning, get out of bed while I was sleeping and leave the house for hours. I admit, I always wondered why you didn't just make up a good lie when you came back. Why didn't you just say, I went to return the movies and ran into an old friend of mine at the video store and he just got this cool new computer, so I went over to check it out and while we were hanging out, his brother-in-law came home from up north where he was diving for abalone and started cooking them up and, have you ever had abalone? It was so good all breaded and fried. And then before I knew it, it was three hours later. Sorry I spaced on calling, honey. You should really meet him sometime. My friend Buck. A good guy.

"Like that," she says. "Why not make something up? You call yourself a good liar?"

"I'm a bad liar," I remind her.

She says, "You lie. But let's roll backwards now. Let's do a little, what do those New Agers call it, a visualization? Why don't you close your eyes?"

"You've got to be kidding," I tell her.

"It was raining pretty hard," she says. "And windy. Do you remember? I was staying at your place because the landlord was gassing my house for rats. You had said, stay with me. Stay here for the weekend, you said. Come on Thursday. It'll be like we live together. You said, It'll be fun. So when I got up to go to work that Friday, you rolled over and said, I'll call you this afternoon. We'll go to dinner. To that new place by the park. Remember?"

"No. Whatever," I say. "What's your point?"

"You never called me that day, but it didn't matter. I'd see you at home, right? You gave me a key. I got off work and I didn't even mind the bus ride over. I remember I sat by the window and the sun had come out. I wore sunglasses on the bus and felt perfectly fine about it. I bought you flowers from that blind lady on the corner and it seemed like I was part of a corny little story. Like, here's the part where I buy a thing of beauty from a woman who only sees darkness. She trusts that I'm putting the right bills in her hand and god, everything is okay. This life, she is good to me."

"Are you on something?" I ask. "Are you high?"

"So, I come back to the apartment and you aren't home yet," she says. "I wasn't worried at all. But this is before I knew you. This is before I knew what you were capable of. I just figured you were running late. Getting your car speakers fixed or whatever it was."

She stops for a second and watches something out on the street below. God, maybe if I just let her use it all up now. Let her talk until she can't speak anymore and maybe she'll never come back.

She laughs and turns around. Her eyes are glassy and that's really the last thing I need. One of her over-the-top crying deals.

"Well, I could really drag this one out," she says. "What I wore, how I eventually put the flowers in a vase and made myself a cocktail. I could go through the round of phone calls I made to your friends, to the restaurant. How I went over and over in my mind the way your mouth formed the name of the restaurant, the way your gray little snaggletooth got caught on your lip when you said it. Just to make sure I hadn't made a mistake. Had I made a mistake?"

"You've made a lot of mistakes," I say, and get up to get a beer.

She just keeps at it while I'm in the kitchen and when I walk back in she's saying, "So I had an idea.

"I had an idea," she says. "I decided to go by the restaurant, thinking maybe our signals got crossed and we were supposed to meet there. When you weren't there, I ran home thinking maybe you'd be there, but you weren't. Then I thought, shit, maybe while I was walking back from the restaurant, you were walking to the restaurant and we crossed paths, so I called the restaurant again but you weren't there. Yet. Maybe you'd be there in a few minutes.

"Okay," she says, looking right at me for the first time. "Do you understand how pathetic this is? Can you even get down with this?"

"Not really," I say. "So I fucked up. I was a big fuck up and so were you. So what? We both knew it wasn't so great."

She laughs and starts playing Chopsticks. "3:30 a.m.," she says. "You came home stinking drunk at 3:30 a.m."

"I believe you were a little looped, too," I say. "To put it mildly."

"Looped?" she shouts. "I was just wrecked, really. Wrecked!"

"Would you mind, you know, keeping it down," I say.

She says, "I said, Where Have You Been This Whole Time? You said, do you remember? You said, I was in Union Square. Not, At A Bar or Having A Drink. Just a general geographical description to really help me out. Smooth move, Ex-Lax!"

She says this like a crazy person. Trilling.

"What's the point?" I say. "It's been years. Can't you just move on?"

"So that night after I calm down a little," she says, "and we're going to bed, you say, I Was Almost Killed Tonight. Do you remember? I Was Almost Killed Tonight. Do you remember a time in your life when you were almost killed?"

I say nothing, this whole scene is hopeless.

"Well, you sure knew just the right thing to say that night. I dropped it after that. Buh-bye," she says. "Buh-bye to all my anger. I wrapped my arms around you and said, My God. I said, What Happened?

"Suddenly, I'm so concerned," she says. "I've been yelling at you about respecting me enough to just call and say you're going to be about, oh, I don't know, nine and a half hours late, but shame on me. Let's all remember our spirits! Get Oprah on the line! I let you off the hook and said, How honey? How did you almost get killed?"

I tell her to get out. I'm on my feet and heading to the door. "Get out now," I say.

"I think you'll want to hear this part," she says. "I think you'll really want to hear this part."

"You have five minutes," I say. "And don't think I won't call the police."

"The police might flip for this story," she says. She's pacing again with her hands clasped behind her back. When did her hands get so huge? She says, "Remember what you said to me? You said you pulled over to check your messages on the way home that night. I parked by the projects, you said. You said, A couple of teenagers started hassling me. They told you to give them your wallet and you told them Fuck You. You said they came toward you and one of them had a gun. I pushed passed him, you said, and got in my car. You kept waiting for him to shoot, you said. But he didn't. The kids stayed by the phone and as you drove away, you pulled onto the sidewalk and pretended like you were going to run them over. You were shaking. You said you scared yourself because you actually thought about killing them. Running them over.

"Oh, sure," she says. "At first I was all wrapped up in your basic human drama. The horror. White man gets harassed by black youths in the city and contemplates killing them. You coming to terms with an awful side of your nature. What has become of us all, etcetera. That thing. And remember what I said first?"

I go to sip my beer, but somehow the can gets twisted around and I dribble on my chin.

"I saw that," she says, narrowing her eyes. "Getting nervous?"

"You're high," I mutter, staring past her head at the wall.

"Listen," she says. "What I said to you was, Why the hell were you checking your messages three blocks from your own house unless you knew you'd fucked up and were supposed to meet me? Why at 3:30 in the morning did you pull over at a fucking pay phone when you were almost home just to see who might have called you?"

I remember that. I remember calling so I could gage how pissed she was going to be when I walked in the door.

"I just really want to see how clearly you remember almost running them over," she says. "Is it clear for you? That you drove up on the sidewalk and then right off again? Without hitting them?"

"I drove up on the sidewalk and just scared them a little," I say. "They were thugs."

"All I'm saying is a couple weeks ago I'm at my friend's house. He's doing this story on the sucky nature of 911 and ambulance service and how it takes forever in some places. I'm looking at this graph, this chart, this list of calls to 911 that never even got answered. I see April 14th. I remember April 14th," she says. "I'll never forget it. This Day In History - Titanic hits an iceberg! U.S. bombs Libya! Lincoln gets assassinated! And it's the birthday of both Loretta Lynn and Anthony Perkins."

And then she folds at the waist like a doll and pops up saying,

"Stand by your psycho fucking man, all right!

"That was April 14th," she says. "I'll never forget it. The day I realized I was dating a lying, cheating, emotionally-wounded opportunist whose hobby was growing ironic facial hair.

"So, some kids called 911 and said some white dude in a green truck, a white guy with a soul patch even. There in the report. In quotes, I think. A white man with a "soul patch." They said a green truck drove up on the sidewalk and hit their friend. Right on that corner where you stopped to check your messages."

"I never hit anybody," I say. "Don't you think I might have noticed if I ran someone down?"

"Oh, nobody's dead," she replies. "Cheer up. One guy just got his femur crushed. Now he gets to be one of those gangsters with a big badass cane. So what, right? It's fashionable, right? They've all got one."

I stand up and push her into the wind tunnel, towards the door.

"All I want is for you to know that I know," she says. "No one else knows. Only me. I haven't told anyone."

"You're leaving now," I say.

"I own it," she says. "I own that part, that story."

She goes out the door and I let her keep walking. I let her just go. I let it happen. I let it go.

Aerosol Halo

I'm inside some strange car, rolling backward down a hill, unable to reach the brakes. Just when the car is truly out of control and I feel like I'm going to crash, I'm suddenly transported. I'm hovering over a party in the desert, doing the dead man's float in the air. It feels glamorous from up here. Is that Chandon they're pouring? It's not until I land, until I sort of touch down and begin walking among the guests, that I realize everyone is wearing those vinyl pants and feather boas from the mall. Maybe I'm not supposed to be this close to them. It looks wrong from here and perhaps I should fly away. The flying part was fun. I start flapping my arms to see if I can do it again. Then there's some weird time lapse, you know how that happens? I look over and see that Jack Nicholson has arrived. He's bouncing up and down on the edge of a cliff laughing and I don't really want to impose myself on him, but since we're both in show business I decide to say, "Hiya, Jack! How's it hanging?"

I can feel static electricity elevating my already-flyaway hair and grab a can of hairspray out of my purse and start spraying. Why am I carrying the leopard print Le Sportsac I had in seventh grade? Didn't I throw it out after that bottle of suntan oil leaked all over it the day I lost my virginity at the beach? Derek Hollis, you bastard.

I feel like I have an aerosol halo. Do I? I look over at Jack again and wonder if he thinks I'm hot. It dawns on me that Jack would probably really like me if he got to know me. "Hiya," I say again. Or maybe this is the first time I'm saying it. Did I say it before or just think it? Jack looks right at me, still bouncing, and goes, "My right testicle is miles above my head and my left one is just a few floors below!"

What is he talking about? I turn around to see if he's talking to someone behind me. I half expect to see one of those fat producers I have never heard of who are always pictured in *Vanity Fair*, but there's no one there. Jeez, I think. That just must be the type of thing that mavericks say. Iconoclasts. It's true, I think. All those magazine articles were right. Some people who work in the system and remain individuals despite the pressure to conform can really get away with whatever they want. Here's my proof.

I run around the party trying to find someone to share this with. I start blurting it out to some blob drinking a Red Bull, but when I look up it's Jack's face I'm saying it to. I say, "Jack Nicholson just told me that..." but it's him. How did that happen? At first I'm worried he'll be angry, but it turns out he is very amused and wants to pal around with me for the rest of the night.

Even in the warm glow of Jack's presence, I snap to my senses. I vow to myself that no matter how right it may seem in the moment, I will not sleep with him. I am not a slut anymore. That was high school. Slowly, I repeat it. You will not succumb to Jack. You will not succumb to Jack. You will not succumb to Jack.

Wait. Can he hear me? Oh my god, I'm thinking out loud.

My eyes pop open and it's still dark. I roll over and squint at the aqua numbers on my Dream Machine clock radio. It's 2:52 a.m. and The Most Important Day of My Life So Far has officially begun. I snap the light on feeling fully awake already. Every moment until the taxi comes has been carefully scheduled and if I get out of bed now, I'll have eight more minutes in the bath.

Sitting on the toilet, I inflate my seashell tub pillow. I pull the plug out of my mouth while wiping and say to myself, "Always multi-tasking."

Don't let anybody tell you I got this job because of my looks, because it's my sense of humor that really hit the homerun. I sink into the warm jasmine-scented water and begin my vocal exercises. "Peas and carrots," I say. "Carrots and peas."

Today, at exactly 6:07 a.m., I will deliver my first solo traffic report for the entire Bay Area. I'm talking all the way out to Contra Costa, not to mention Solano County. Hercules, the Dumbarton Bridge, even Benicia. A lot of people complain that the area has sprawled so far, we're just one long housing subdivision to the state's capital (Sacramento, Pop. 1,929,403 and growing!) but I see it differently. It feels like we're all coming together.

Just one year ago, fresh out of Chico State with a psychology degree, I got a job at KPID-TV as the advertising receptionist. I didn't use any connections even though that's what everybody thinks. I just went in there and nailed my interview, feeling extra confident in a brand new green tea-colored skirt and eggshell sailor's blouse. After the station manager, Grant Davis Hildritch III, glanced over my resume which, besides school, only listed my part-time cashier job at The Cookie Pantry and a stint at telemarketing, selling tickets to the Santa Clara County Firefighters' Rodeo, he offered me a piece of bubblegum from his desktop bubblegum machine. He put a penny in it and cranked the wheel, extending his huge palm with the little blue orb set in it like a jewel.

"Carmela," he said. "Allow me to offer you a gumball."

I thought about declining because it seemed unprofessional, like maybe it was some kind of test. You know, will she or won't she? And you know what? I decided to take it because I wanted a chance to show my fun side. Bubblegum is fun. Bubblegum shows you still have a little bit of the kid left in you. My college roommates always teased me about being too serious, but I can still get a little wild sometimes. Just last month I went to that bar in SOMA where people dance on the tables at last call and, you guessed it, I got up there and really let loose, too. And for Halloween a few years ago I went all out and dressed up as a French maid. Hello?

When Grant gave me this latest promotion to traffic reporter on *Bay Expressions*, he said, "I'll never forget the first day you came in to interview. I knew you were going to go far after you took that bubblegum. The way you blew those bubbles showed me you had spunk. You're a go-getter."

I won't deny it. Just the other day I looked up my alumni website on the internet and a lot of the people from the communications department are still interning in newsrooms or working for small radio stations. I say, why not get paid to learn something new every day? For instance, just about a month ago while in the KPID cafeteria I heard Silicon Valley correspondent Stacey Ramirez say to noon anchor Donna Corkindale, "Hey, Donna. If I knew you were doing that feature on the sanitation department, I would have teased it on my clusterbump." I started blushing, but I knew there had to be a logical explanation. I ran into Grant's office, why not start at the top, and asked him all about teases and clusterbumps. And now look at me. I'm in a dressing room at the Bay Area's top television station looking at myself in one of those mirrors with all the lightbulbs surrounding it. They're like petals to the flower that is me. I smooth down my chestnut bob with my palms and practice a few lines.

"The Bay Bridge is backed up through the MacArthur Maze and the metering lights are still on." I furrow my brow a tinge. "Runaway big rig," I say. "Fender bender." And then for kicks, "Wayward mattress." (Don't laugh. It happens.) I take a lint brush to my cafe au lait-colored pantsuit saying, "And I'm Carmela Cook for KPID Traffic."

Soon enough, I'm saying it for real on the air. You should have seen me soaring across the blue screen, citing a non-injury accident on the Highway 17 summit with a quick slice of my baton. And when I got to the stall on northbound 880 near Whipple Road, I even remembered to thank Mr. Vitas Choudhary of Menlo Park for tipping us off on the 24-hour KPID Good Sam hotline. When I handed it back over to Steve and Summer, they were stunned. I could see it in their faces. My first time on air and it came off like I'd been doing it my entire life.

I refueled at the station's juice bar with an Orange Mango Zippy with a Booster of ChromoGinseng and my next three segments that morning went even better. By 9 a.m. the calls and emails were flooding in. Everyone loved me! I even had my first marriage proposal. When I got to the dressing room, Grant had seven gorgeous calla lilies waiting for me with a note that said, "The Bay Area's News Leader Just Got Better!" Isn't that sweet?

My popularity grows more and more every day. And it's not just the usual stuff like men wanting to go out on dates. Women want to have coffee with me. Grandmothers want to make me sweaters. Teenage girls write in saying they want to be me when they grow up. In the morning paper they called it Carmela Mania and quoted my childhood friends and my parents. I am the Bay Area's

Commute Queen with girl-next-door charm and a "sexy sibilance" when I report on the ferry from Sausalito to San Francisco. The caption under the photo said, "Legs like a racehorse and brainy to boot. Who is traffic's wondergirl?"

Grant called me into his office the other morning and wanted to make sure all this attention wasn't going to my head.

"Carmela," he said, "I know you're all that and everybody else thinks you're all that, too. But as soon as you find yourself strutting down the street on a gorgeous afternoon, wind blowing through your hair, wearing some revealing little number that cost too much and makes you look cheap, and you're thinking, 'Hey, I am all that!' that's when it's curtains for you. You are loved because you look like you really want to be loved. As you start projecting to the citizens of the Bay Area that you have enough love, the love will cease. Do you understand?"

"Yes, Mr. Hildritch," I replied.

"Keep calling me Grant, dolly. An old fart needs special little nuggets, too."

I tried even harder to be humble. Given everything we know about television and movie stars, like Barbra Streisand for number one, there were too many examples out there to warn me away from getting a big head. I can't imagine demanding that my dressing room be carpeted in white shag or that fresh rose petals be sprinkled into the toilet before I do a number two.

But things changed around the station. Some of the anchors even started to get jealous and wouldn't talk to me anymore. Anchors with twenty years of experience, who know the ins and outs of local news better than anyone else, were suddenly giving me the cold shoulder. I pretended not to notice. When Jean O'Hara from weather told me it looked like my hips were getting a little big, I just told her, "Oh, I know. It's all that chocolate I'm getting from my fans. I'd better watch it," even though I knew it wasn't true. If I were in a movie, I'd probably look her right in the eye and I'd be taller than her with a bigger bustline (which is the truth in reality anyway) and I'd say, "You know what, Jean? Traffic is the new weather! Weather is so last year," and the door would open right on cue, and she'd stand there stunned as I stepped into my Lincoln Towncar.

My job became more challenging every day because, in addition to my reports, I was making appearances at youth functions and station-sponsored barbecues. I met so many of my fans at mall openings and car washes that it really kept me humble. I'll never forget the day that Rosemary Ternthwat of Livermore came up to me at the Chinese New Year Parade and said, "You remember me, don't you, Carmela?" And for the life of me, I couldn't remember where we met. She stomped off only to return a few minutes later, tears streaming down her face, yelling, "You fucking cunt! You showed up to present my father with a medal at his retirement party from the police department and now he's dead! Dead! And you don't even care, standing there with your hooker makeup and that red satin Suzy Wong dress. You've forgotten who made you what you are!"

Even though a lot of people who witnessed the scene came up to me afterwards and said, "Hey, no way was that your fault, Carmela. Some people just expect too much from celebrities!" I still know that I never, ever wanted that to happen again.

I started keeping a running log of the people I met at what function every night before I went to bed. Maybe a little physical description, too. Like a flashcard for important people. The system worked pretty well, I just brushed up about an hour a day, and soon it became one of the things I was known for.

The schedule became so hectic, but I was anything but a quitter. Even though bits of my hair started to fall out in chunks, I kept on cutting those ribbons and getting my photo taken with city officials and handicapped kids. Who could sleep when there were parades and film festivals and triathlons to go to?

Pretty soon weather started getting bumped down a minute or two every night, so that I could send out special birthday messages to my fans. Jean O'Hara quit and was replaced by a bitter stand-up comedian with a drinking problem who always pinched my behind when I walked by. I laughed it off. I got used to it just like I got used to checking for whoopie cushions and chewed-up gum before I sat down at my dressing table. I really had no choice.

During ratings week, they decided to have me start doing traffic on the evening news even though there weren't so many commute concerns for me to pay attention to. Occasionally there was a crash or a fire, but mostly I would just give a rundown on what freeways were clear and what we could expect to see tomorrow. After that, I got approached by the Cleveland market and the greater Dallas-Fort Worth area, but I really felt that after only six months here there was so much more to learn. And for a bonus, I got a free weekend at Grant's lodge in Tahoe. But more than any bonus or perk, I just wanted to do a good job alerting people to the traffic concerns of the seven county area.

But things felt like they were caving in all around me. My reports were still fine, but whenever I would congratulate a couple from Milpitas on their 35th anniversary, an angry call would come in from the kids of some couple in Santa Rosa. "We thought you'd come through for us, Carmela!" I tried so hard, but the more I tried to do, it seemed like the more I was failing. I started sleeping only four hours a night, drifting off with my pile of flashcards.

Still I received lots of positive feedback and presents, but the negativity was increasing more everyday. One afternoon after a particularly scathing email in which Mr. Andrew Folger of Emeryville listed off my hair and makeup blunders for the past twelve newscasts, I went into Grant's office.

"I can't take it anymore, Grant," I said, clutching at a few strands of my hair and letting them wisp toward the air filter.

"Dolly," he said. "We've been waiting for this."

"You were?" I said. I felt terrible that they had noticed me flailing.

"And honestly, we thought this day would come a lot sooner." He threw a penny in the machine on his desk and said, "Gumball?"

I had just brushed my teeth, but plucked the yellow gum from his palm and set about chewing slowly, working it around my mouth with a quiet determination. No bubbles today, I'm afraid.

He got up and shut the door. He said that even though there had been an upper management meeting prompted by Mr. Folger's concerns about my appearance, he had a master plan as long as I promised not to wear any more orange.

"That viewer was right, you know," he said. "It really does give your skin a strange pallor."

"What's your plan for me, Grant?" My eyes were stinging with tears. "What are we going to do with me?"

Grant said the station had ties with cable networks. They wanted to give me my own show. A program bringing together the winning triumvirate of Carmela, traffic, and the people who love us both.

I could hardly breathe. I had always assumed that I wanted to travel up the ladder doing traffic and commuting until one day it dawned on me that I wouldn't be able to go national. There's no national commuting report! What had I been thinking? I had started in one of the biggest markets in the country and now that I had conquered that, what else was left?

"Think about it, Carmela," Grant said gently. "The Weather Channel does all right, doesn't it?"

I swallowed the hard lump of gum and felt the room expand

by the second. The earth was huge. There were people traveling everywhere.

Mass Theft

Mr. Grant Davis Hildritch III
Station Manager
KPID TV
2002 Van Ness Avenue
San Francisco, CA 94103

Dear Mr. Hildritch:

I was told your name by the receptionist at your office. This is a very urgent letter and I pray you read it and take action immediately. This story is not only for all Bay Areans, but for residents of the whole world. I have been WRONGED and someone needs to get to the bottom of it quick. I will offer 50% reward money on all returned profits from my recording career, movie career and all monies that are owed to me by Bill Gates. You or someone else could be a millionaire.

First please read my rundown on how I was successful in recording, movies and computers to determine that I am for real.

When I was eight years old, I was almost a master of the violin. I attended all the famous music schools and by the time I was eleven I was sitting in with the likes of Popol Vuh and Yes. For the next twenty years of my life, I sat in with bands of this caliber and even higher. This music is mostly called "progressive rock" or "prog rock" and I am an expert about it.

Even though I was a world-class player, I knew I would not be able to make a decent living as a violin player in prog rock bands and I began a new career path. There was something called computers and I was very interested in learning more about it. Wouldn't you know I was in the same classes as a man who later became known as Bill Gates? (So you are not confused, his name back then was Bill Gates, too, but I just meant that now the WORLD knows him as Bill Gates.)

During the time I studied computer science, I also was sitting in with the major prog rock bands that were touring the greater Boston area. This included Starbender, which was an offshoot of one of the guys of Emerson, Lake and Palmer. I think it was Lake.

This information should all be verifiable. You will have to agree that this information leads one to believe that I had a good chance for making a lot of money in either the music industry or the computer industry.

Then there was my excellent skill at Tae Kwon Do (MARTIAL ARTS) which led me to a career as a bodyguard for many Hollywood celebrities. What I am saying here is that with all that money around you could guess that someone has started using amnesia-producing drugs in order for people to be tricked out of their money. Tom Cruise and Julia Roberts make around $20 mil PER PICTURE. Do you not think that with this type of money there are people who are willing to do very illegal things to get at it? Below is the list of my mass theft case. At first it seems unbelievable, but if you do some research you will be able to see that I am not making this up. I have just lost a lot of my memory due to amnesia drugs I was given. By whom, I do not know.

Four to eight years ago I made a lot of money writing parts of national software packages, scripts for movies, advisor positions, and playing concerts. I have also been left money in people's wills that I don't remember getting paid for. I even spotted some houses recently that I think I owned. If I split this money with whoever helps me collect, there could be more that ten million in it for each of us.

I am fingerprinting all of my letters and I would like to remind anyone thinking of intercepting this letter that interfering with the federal mail is a federal offense.

Thank you.

Bradley Welch - 546-291-7539
4609 Hollingway Ave. #C
Quincy, MA 02169

Houses I believe I am supposed to own include :
789 Terrence Court, Bedford, IN
3743 E. Azalia Ave., Albuquerque, NM
1609 Middlebury Rd., Brockton, MA
477 Dwight Rd., Brockton, MA
7200 29th Ave., Denver, CO (I received this house for writing part

of the film "Murphy's Romance")
also possible homes in Malibu? Studio City? Lake Tahoe??

Cars I believe I am supposed to own include:
1994 Camaro – GRN 804
1992 Jeep Grand Cherokee -16RT455
1992 Lexus or Infiniti – TYU6322
1986 Cadillac – LOP 939

Microsoft software I helped write:
Access 95
BackOffice Server 4.0
Excel 2000
Links 97
Advised Microsoft with Karen Thiesson on Windows 95. For this I received 1.74 million dollars, which was afterwards stolen. Karen Thiesson is unavailable for comment.

Main plots I wrote:
Judge Dredd (In addition to writing most of the main plot to this movie I also played a member of the main jury and I wrote a little of the computer graphics at the very end.) Paid 84K(?) which was afterwards stolen.
A Perfect World – Never paid.
Tango & Cash – Never paid.
He Said, She Said - I wrote about 1/4 of this on location and will probably not be paid.
Money Train – Woody Harrelson was in this and will remember me, but I can't get through to him.
The Last Boy Scout – Never paid. I also staged the main fight scene in the movie's beginning.
Terminal Bliss – Never paid.

Under Siege - Mr. Seagal knows about my 40K. Speak up, Mr. Seagal!!

Wyatt Earp - It took me an amazingly long time to remember I wrote about 50 % of this main plot and was one of the extras.

Advisor positions:

Ghost - I advised that they should cast Whoopi Goldberg.

Hoffa - I staged one fight scene for which I was never paid.

Naked Gun 33 1/3: The Final Insult - afterwards stolen.

Die Hard: With a Vengeance - afterwards stolen.

Single White Female - This advisor position that I did almost nothing on was supposed to pay well.

Nick of Time - Johnny Depp tripped over my head in this movie.

Kalifornia - Never paid.

Mr. Wonderful - I contribute almost nothing to this movie, but did request 10K for two days of my time. Never paid.

Devil in a Blue Dress - I suggested that Denzel Washington smoke Mexican cigarettes.

Concerts:

Rush - A full concert tour for 65K is what I remember. All money was paid to me and was afterwards stolen.

Frank Zappa - A few concerts. Never paid.

The Stone Roses - Violin on one song for eight-city tour. Never paid.

Anita Baker - Never paid.

Grateful Dead - I gave Bob Weir a 40K check to reform the band with me in it. If the band was not reformed with me in it, the 40k was to be given back to me. Money never returned.

Recordings:

Loggins and Messina - Violin for tribute record. Never paid.

Whitney Houston – Arrangements for The Bodyguard. Ms. Houston, speak up.

Co-writer for the theme song to Death Becomes Her. Never paid.

Muppets Christmas record. Paid 5K, afterwards stolen.

Wills:

CIA Agent – Sandra Price who was murdered willed me 10K, which was afterwards stolen.

Hugh Brannun aka Mr. Greenjeans from Captain Kangaroo willed me over 200K, which was later stolen.

Television:

I was a man with an unknown tumor on ER for a feature scene. The 2K was stolen.

I co-produced one episode of Roseanne. Roseanne Barr Arnold is denying she knows me.

I made one brief appearance on Murder She Wrote. Paid - afterward stolen.

I seem to remember a television pilot called Milligan. If this aired, I was Milligan. Never paid?

I seem to remember an appearance on the David Letterman Show with Grover Washington, Jr. and Toni Braxton. Donald Sutherland was the main guest. Never paid.

I was Bingo on The Banana Splits for two episodes.

Advisor to the X-Files episode where Jeremiah Smith is the link to the colonization plan and the one where the security guard is found frozen to death. Was there an episode with a brown bear? David Duchovny, feel free to respond. Never paid.

Miscellaneous

Did I receive 1 million from Ted Turner for referring computer specialists to TBS?

Did Microsoft give me any complimentary computers that were later stolen?

Did I fight Steven Seagal in a tournament that was for NBC but never aired?

It is unbelievable and sad that there are so many thieves in the world. Please help me get my money back. You will be given a reward of 50% of the recovered money when the thieves are brought to justice. Thank you for your time. Please contact me if you need more details for your investigation.

What You're Worth

Casey got a new girlfriend pronto. I, on the other hand, sit here with a slow healing coccyx and a constant ringing in my left ear. A bad accident I will probably tell you about in a minute. All that really matters is somehow I have turned into a chain-snacking, t.v. watching loner. Part of the problem. One of those people that the masses angrily rail against on public radio. As a lifelong Republican and former big game hunter, I am used to a certain segment of the population not rushing to embrace me, but nothing cries out for scorn better than an antisocial prematurely gray middle-aged woman with a seventeen-hour-a-day television addiction who hasn't taken out her garbage in two months.

At least I've got myself on a normal person's schedule again. I think it's the first step in my recovery. No all-nighters. No eating eggs, waffles or other typical breakfast foods except for breakfast. No more of my seven hour "naps" during the day. Now I wake up bright and early when my next door neighbor's alarm goes off. The walls here suck. He's got some set up where his alarm sound is that line from *Blazing Saddles* where Richard Pryor says, "Where are all the white women at?!" He usually gets it on the third or fourth time, does some sit-ups or something, and gets in the shower. They all shower in the morning. All five apartments. They shower, listen to music. I can hear modems dialing and connecting. I make my pot of coffee and turn on the local morning show while they do all this. I like to think I'm having my coffee with them. That we're all having coffee together, it's just that we're adult enough to enjoy it in the privacy of our own homes. We don't need to talk about it. Doors slam, people trudge down the stairs. Sometimes they run into each other in the hall and say hello. Sometimes I can tell there's two people in the hall, but they don't say anything that I can hear. They just walk out the front door and they're on their way, leaving me to hold down the fort. I'm the boss here and they don't even know it.

Jesus, hell, there's been a situation here, okay? I did not mean to drop the crate of eggs on the floor of the bakery's walk-in refrigerator, nor did I expect as I swiped at the slop with a filthy T-shirt that a large metal beam would mysteriously dislodge itself from the ceiling and come crashing down on my backside. It's been a long haul from the moment three months ago when I lay on the freezing cement floor waiting for help to come to today when I realized there was something to live for again. Now that I'm on the road to becoming a decent person again, it seems hard to imagine that for a long time all I really wanted to do was go on a shooting spree.

That night in the ER, nobody could find Casey, who was technically my spouse. We were married in a mass wedding ceremony in Hawaii last year and turns out the whole time I was being cheated on with a stripper named (are you ready?) Kitten. That's not even her stage name either. Her stage name is something that really stands out among all those Ambers and Destinys and Colettes. Something like Liz or Barb, I think. Anyway, Casey'd drop me off for my swing baking shift, pick the little tramp up at the Century, and stay with her all night. Then it was off to the day job at a silkscreening warehouse and afterwards coming home and taking a short nap with me, before getting up and going out again. Fucking speed. Let's hear it for copious amounts of meth.

When Casey finally straggled into the hospital the next day, totally wigging, it was like I could see it all so clear. Like that metal pole knocked some sense into me. I said, "Don't let the door hit you on the ass and be sure to take your goddamn iguana." There was no need to process. Last month, one of my old co-workers called to say she spotted Casey hanging out with a bunch of crackheads on Turk St. Looked pretty bad, I guess. Supposedly sporting a really bad bleach job and wearing one of those half-wetsuits. A full wetsuit would have been enough, but one of those with the shorts and short sleeves? It was too much. I just said thanks and hung up. I tried to act as if she was alerting me to something minor and informative. Like there was a new laundromat that just opened down the street that stayed open till 2 a.m. where the 50 lb. washers only cost a buck. Okay, thanks, I said. I'll keep that in mind.

My ex-lover is a crackhead in a half-wetsuit and my new love is my t.v. We couldn't watch t.v. when I was a kid, and for a long time I believed all that hype about t.v. being bad. I've discovered that t.v. is actually a pretty stupendous invention that brings pleasure to my life. I won't outline my whole schedule here, it's complicated, a lot of surfing, but just know it's not all talk shows and I don't watch a single soap opera. I have a thing for the ones where judges really sock it to people and I also love ones with animals I've never seen in person before. The highlight of my day, though, has to be 2 p.m. when the girl at the deli downstairs brings me up my lunch and I eat it along with *Circus of Antiques*. I'm sure you've seen it now that it's turned into what the staff at *TV Guide* calls "a runaway hit." People from all walks of life bring down furniture and paintings and moldy curiosities and these pros evaluate them. Yesterday this lady from Dallas found out her great aunt's death certificate was worth a bundle because the coroner who signed it turned into a serial killer later. I've already done a twice over of all my stuff, preparing for when the *Circus* comes here, but I quickly realized I don't have anything worthwhile. I'm not going to be like some of those people who bring garbage and think they're going to make a million.

Who are those people who flock to the show bearing quilts and photographs and weaponry? I've never met these kind of people. Where in the world do they get these African hunting trophies, Civil War field paintings and rare *Star Wars* action figures? I mean, a Han Solo doll with Princess Leah's breasts? Still in its original packaging? My mother never taught me about any of this. If I had just learned all about this stuff earlier, I could have started snatching things up at the Queen of Apostles rummage sale when I was a kid in Modesto. I would have gone to garage sales instead of playing softball. There were probably little important things all around me and I passed over them. I always thought everything was junk.

Maybe you've heard of this thing called "shabby chic." This is a real expression used for interior decorating and I'm not kidding. That's what I say I've got when I'm thinking to myself how I would describe my place if someone ever asked. It's pretty much a stained couch with a blanket thrown over it, a coffee table with fake marble inlays and a big inflatable ball that you can sit on. Come to think of it, the ball was sort of a find.

I was walking back from the bus stop one day when I heard somebody yelling, "Hey, dude. Dude! Catch!" I looked up and some kids in an office, some web company called RaiseTheRoof.com, were tossing these things out the window at everybody. It was either a promotional thing because they just opened or they were going out of business and getting rid of everything. I never figured it out, but I kept the ball just because. You need some balance to make it work for you, it's just a ball after all, so I never sit on it.

Casey took all of the posters and wall stuff upon moving out, except for the picture of Half Dome, which is pretty and all, but honestly, I just don't care for wall decorations too much. It's such a statement about yourself. I Like This. I Like Half Dome. I never understood the point of making a statement about yourself to yourself. If you like the Sydney Opera House or puppies or Picasso so much, why would you need to remind yourself? Every time you pass by the dreamcatcher in your hallway, do you think, I Like That. I Like My Dreamcatcher. Pretty soon you'd stop even seeing it and then, what's the point?

This is also why I never got tattoos. Even though I told people earlier in my life that it was because I wanted to stay clean so I'd never have any identifying marks for the cops, I just never understood it. Don't you know what you like or what you want to remember without the constant reminders that never let up? That you can never turn off? And if you need the constant reminders, maybe you should be forgetting this shit after all. Maybe you don't need it. Do you want the person sitting down next to you on the train or standing in line behind you at the drugstore to get part of your story? To me, it's like looking at a car with bumperstickers. I'd rather not know anything about you at all and yet, there you are. A red Ford Focus with a dented wheel well supporting Judy Rothberg for El Cerrito City Council. There you are, you gay Trans Am, imparting that the goddess is afoot. Hey, it's another frosty green Beetle suggesting that we Free Tibet and stop in at the Anderson Valley Brewing Company in Boonville for a Boont Amber. People in their skins seem like plenty to me. But then there are all the hearts with the banners to contend with. The anchors, the flowers, the angels, the bombshells, the Nike swooshes, and the flames, all the flames, everything is on fire, burn it all down. It's gotten too noisy, which is why I can't leave the house.

Yesterday morning after everyone in the building was gone I was tuning into *Bay Expressions*, the morning show. They've got this very attractive traffic gal now and even though I'm a bonafide shut-in, I like to catch her segments. I like to mentally map out where I would avoid if I were trying to get somewhere.

It's a good thing I don't have to drive all the way over the Carquinez Bridge because of that chemical spill, I'd think to myself while fixing up a fried egg sandwich. Thank god I am here and not backed up on the Idylwild turn-off.

So Carmela the traffic lady has just finished her second installment when I start hearing this drip up above. Like the ceiling in the apartment above me was leaking onto the floor. As I said, our walls are thin here and we've got all sorts of problems in the bathrooms with plaster flaking off. Supposedly the guy next door has a big old hole in his bathroom ceiling and can see the bottom of #4's bathtub. I turn up the volume, but I still hear the little tick of it hitting every couple of seconds. We all know how this is. I'm not saying I'm special because this happened to me, it's just that I can barely concentrate on the show is all. Just call the landlady, a sane person might suggest. Well, in the five years I've been here we've had leaks, fires, and a pigeon infestation, and never did she show her face. There's a maintenance guy I could page, but he's pure trouble. A drunk with a dirty mind and a temper, just like someone else I know. That's the worst kind of drunk if you ask me. No thanks. A person can really go far just by avoiding people like this. For every piece of scum you avoid, you move ahead a little bit more.

Here comes the *Circus*! Just hearing the theme music makes my heart race a little. My tuna melt and chips have arrived right on schedule and I settle in for my hour-long slice of heaven. You should have seen this kid with a whole bundle of old rock and roll posters. Terry, my very favorite appraiser, sort of a wiry no-b.s. guy, takes a look at the stash and says, "Interesting indeed, but what's all this writing on the back?" The kid gives him some nonsense about writing his name on them so no one could rip him off. He wrote on the posters with permanent ink! Boy, you should have seen Terry's expression. It was priceless. Of course, the value just plummeted. And right there in the moment Terry tells him how much they would have been worth if they were totally mint, I mean, I wanted an instant replay! I've got to get a VCR to record these. Besides that, everything else on the episode was pretty standard. Some rugs with patterns of Belgian royalty, an old snuff box and a pretty choice spittoon.

The minute the show's over, the drip comes back louder than ever. I can't take it anymore. There's no way I can wait until she gets home and calls someone, so I decide to take some action. I grab a pot from the stack in the sink, my Blockbuster card and a screwdriver, and open my front door. "Here comes trouble!" I say out loud. Seeing no one in the hall, I head up the stairs to #6 and do a little rat-a-tat-tat on the door. I am sure no one is there, but I go through the formalities anyway. "Knock-knock-knock," I say while I knock.

"Anybody home?" I say, reaching for the handle. Locked, of course, but I know full well this lady never comes home until eight or so. Back in the days when I traveled up and down the state with this group of radical women firefighters, we had to do this lockpicking shit all the time. And under intense pressure. I grab my kit out of my sweatpants' waistband and set to work. The thing is jimmied in about ten seconds flat. I suppose I've still got it.

I take a few steps back and push open the door and, I swear, if I hadn't just walked up the stairs from my place, I'd think I was in a completely different apartment building. The ceilings in here are at least three feet higher than mine and instead of white walls, they're painted really light blues and greens. I almost feel like I'm underwater. Could she have done all this herself? Why would anybody fix up a rental place? Just when you get it where you want it, they're going to pull it out from under you. I couldn't help but feel a little sorry for how stupid she was.

I moved my toes around on the waxy, wooden floor, which, I might add, you could eat off. Not a dustbunny in sight. I surveyed the place for a second, not moving. I'll admit to you that I entertained the thought of snooping into the bedroom and bathroom to see how it stacked up in there, but then I heard the drip. Right there in front of me was a puddle spreading out like, well it reminded me of urine, and I put the pot down in it. It made the puddle spread out even further and I figured maybe I should wipe it up. I wasn't going to use one of her towels, though I imagined she had a big stack of fluffy ones around here somewhere. I didn't want to go all the way back downstairs, so I peeled off my socks and swooshed them around a bit. A drop hit me on the head and then I replaced the pot and waited for the next drop to fall. A couple seconds later, the next one hit and I knew then and there that the sound of the drops hitting the metal wasn't going to do at all. I threw the wet socks in the pot to buffer the noise and went back down to catch Judge Ratchett and take care of this runaway toenail I just noticed.

Around six I heard someone in the hall and panicked. I bolted up off the couch and ran to listen at the door. It sounded like that top-heavy Chinese guy in #5, not whatsername, but I took it as a sign. I figured I'd better get up there and collect the pot sooner rather than later. I put on some new socks because I think that socks are quieter than bare feet, aren't they? I've always assumed that. I hadn't bothered locking her door again and walked right on in. I picked up the pot and took a look inside. "Maybe I'll have sock soup for dinner," I said to myself. All this excitement was really bringing my sense of humor back. I laughed out loud just to seal the deal.

As I started to walk out, something caught my eye. This lady had shelves and shelves of bric-a-brac and tiny trinkets. The whole north wall was floor to ceiling shelves. A bunch of dolls, tiny framed black and white photos of old people, a big blue vase and some music boxes, but out of it all there was one thing that stood out. Sitting there, as if it was in a spotlight, the star of the whole show, was a little cookie tin. It's like when you're sitting on the bus and you see somebody's shoes and you think, "Those are some really nice shoes," and then you realize they caught your eye because you have the exact same pair.

But I didn't have this cookie tin. This cookie tin, this very one sitting in front of me now, was featured on *Circus of Antiques* a few weeks ago. I'm positive. It was from the Royal Wedding of Prince Charles and Lady Di, and Terry had said it was worth at least three big ones! I'm sure this lady has no idea she's sitting on a gold mine. It happens all the time I've learned. A lot of people have no idea what they're holding onto and that's why it just blows my mind that people don't get these things checked out. Is she living in a hole? There's no way she hasn't heard of the *Circus*, some of the star appraisers (including Terry) were just profiled on *That's Entertainment For You* two weeks ago! I would've imagined that anyone who has anything would have looked into it by now.

At first I was scared to touch it. What if I devalued it somehow by touching it? It definitely looked like the real McCoy. Little heads of them both inside tiny ovals, the crest, everything. For maybe a split second I thought about swiping it, but before I knew it I was locking the door behind me and padding down the stairs with my potful of soggy socks.

I must have dozed off on the couch because the eleven o'clock news was on and the drip was gone. I dreamed that I was up in her apartment scooting around in circles on my butt. With every circle, I got closer and closer to the tin. When I lifted my arm up to grab it, I couldn't reach it. My hand was patting around on the shelf, but nothing seemed to be there. My back hurt too much to stand up, so I just willed it down telekinetically and wore it as a crown for awhile.

Hail is hitting the window now. It looks like morning. Now usually my first thought of the day is always my friend Mr. Coffee and the piping hot gift he brings, but today I woke up thinking about the tin. I sit up and try to bring the blood into my feet by pounding them with a little contraption called The Bonger. By the way, The Bonger is a modern invention I can really get behind. Whoever thought of this, a rubber ball on the end of a flexible piece of metal you kind of slap yourself around with to increase circulation, that's the brand of genius I like. I bong away on my calves for awhile and start thinking how you couldn't hit the tin with The Bonger. It would dent for sure. Jesus. It all keeps coming back to the tin. I might just have to pay it a visit today.

I flip on the t.v. and see it's only 5:45 a.m. She doesn't leave for work until around 8:30, so if I'm going to do it, I've got a lot of time to kill. *Bay Expressions* isn't even on yet, so I watch an exercise show for awhile. Go for the burn. Work it out. Remember to breathe.

All those thighs moving around, the arms and legs flying, sort of lull me into a daydream. I think about how maybe I should just wait it out, be patient. This could turn out to be a real downward spiral if I don't watch it. Maybe one morning I'll wake up and all her old junk will be out in boxes on the curb. She'll move out like they all do. Even after the homeless people have picked through the soiled bedsheets and warped cassette tapes, the tin will still be there for me. My body will be all healed by then and I'll tap dance up like Shirley Temple to pluck out my grand prize.

Maneuvers

I didn't even have to audition. You'd think that they'd at least want to hear a story about where you grew up or have you tell your most embarrassing moment. Just to see how you'll do in front of the cameras. It's not acting or anything, but it's something. It would say something about a person for sure.

First, it was pretty weird because I spent all morning getting dressed and doing my hair and makeup and I take the bus out to Concord and wait in the huge line and all that happened was they take a Polaroid of me. They just put me in front of a wall and snapped one shot, had me write my name and number on it and then they sent me away. I would have been pretty p.o.'ed about it, but the next day they called! Now I get to go back again tomorrow. This is called getting a callback.

I'll have to take another afternoon off from Villa Sereno, but Marjorie is the nicest boss ever. She said if I make it on the show, they will just hire a temporary person from the Russell Hobson Center until I get back. They should hire Judy. She is my best friend from the RH Center and is in a wheelchair. It's not a big deal or anything. She could do everything I do, like passing out the medicines or bringing dinners or buttering rolls. She is really smart and hasn't let the fact she can't walk stop her. Way to be, Judy!

The show I will be on if I make it is called *Maneuvers*, by the way. It's a new one done by the same guys who did both *Raider* and *Roommates*. I'm a total *Raider* fanatic since the first season and pretty much like *Roommates*, too. *Roommates* is the one that's all about people in a big city. I think it must be New York. This one house has to select a roommate out of all these people who come and try out. Some people are gay and some people have shaved heads and some people play the guitar. I can't tell if the person ever goes to live with them. They don't show that part. They just show all the strangers trying to get accepted into the house every week.

I would never try out for *Roommates*. I know I would get rejected right off the bat and I don't need all of America laughing at me. America likes to make fun of people on t.v. If I was blind or deaf or couldn't walk, everyone would know it wasn't right to laugh. With me, it's just all these little things added up together. My talking is a little off even though I made a lot of improvement in my speech therapy. My arms are kind of short. Sometimes, it takes me awhile to do reading, but I am okay at math stuff. Plus I have a lot of scars from acne when I was a teenager. Right now I am saving up my money to get a treatment where they peel off your skin with chemicals or lasers even though that is sort of unnecessary. I know I am a lucky person and have a lot to be thankful for.

When I heard about how *Maneuvers* was looking for people,

at first I wasn't going to do it. At first I thought it would be only for certain people because it is very physical and deals with military strategies and secret things for spies. The thing is they need regular people, too. It said "everyday people" in the ad and I was like, "yessss!" When I got to the auto parts store and saw all the other people lined up, I was pretty nervous. There were so many really pretty girls. A lot of girls looked like Tabitha Fallows in the "I Feel You" video where she is wearing the pink bodysuit and gets to fly like a flying princess. It made me get a bit down about my chances. Then I saw how they weren't treated any different from me. Except for this one girl with extra big earrings who got to go inside the trailer because she fainted, everyone else got only a Polaroid taken of them, too. I heard some of the girls saying the other one faked fainting, but it looked real to me. Why would you fake hitting the hard concrete and getting your knees all bloody?

Now it is after the callback day and first let me say that I wore my red cowboy boots. I read in a magazine somewhere that it's a good idea to wear something the director will remember you by. If this thing works for you, it can become what they call your signature item. If you want to know, I could soon become the girl in the red cowboy boots to the whole U. S. of A because I got picked! I GOT PICKED! Can you believe it?

Okay, there was one more round where I was asked a whole bunch of questions about what I like to do and what my family is like and what my job is, but I passed it with flying colors. They asked me if I had a boyfriend and I said, No way! because you're supposed to tell the truth and I have never had a boyfriend and I don't want one. After I said this, the interview was over and they told me I passed the test! This really nice lady called Georgie who totally looked exactly like the reporter from the show Downtown Girls with the hair and all said she would call me the next day to talk about the details.

I go home and tell my parents about the whole thing at supper. They are so happy for me because I have tried a few times to get on game shows and they have been so nice about supporting me and I have never gotten anything before now. After we do the dishes, we get on the phone and call everybody to tell them the good news. I call Marjorie from work and she is really proud. She says that I shouldn't worry about my job at the center. They will hold it for me for the six weeks until the show finishes taping out in the desert.

It's not that I'm in too bad of shape, but I know *Maneuvers* is going to be a lot of physical exercise. I started on my push-ups and sit-ups tonight in my bedroom to get a head start. Dad tells me to settle down after awhile cause they're trying to sleep, so I slip under the covers and practice holding my breath in case there is swimming involved.

I wore my red cowboy boots to work, which I have never done. All the clients have heard the news and when I walk in, everyone in the day room gives me a round of applause. Marjorie leads them in a Hip Hip Hooray and even the really old people like Myrna and Lou seem happy for me. First thing I have to get used to is everyone calling me Movie Star now.

"Hey, Movie Star!" Chucky says in the kitchen. "Are you going to get too big for your britches down in Hollywood and never come back?"

"It's not in Hollywood, Chucky!" I say. "It's a nowhere place in the middle of the desert."

Sheesh, I can't believe this is going to last another week until I start the show. It's embarrassing!

Of course I'm going to come back to Villa Sereno. I might get to do a few talk shows afterwards if I'm lucky, but I am not going to be like a lot of those people from the reality shows. Every time I see one of them acting like they belong at a movie premiere or trying to fit in with real stars, I feel so bad for them. I can spot the difference between a famous star and someone from a reality t.v. show a mile away. Everyone can. I will be proud to take my six weeks of fame and settle with that.

Fast forward to the night before I leave. I've been doing exercises all week and walking to and from work instead of letting Mom drive me. The producer people told me I wouldn't need too many civilian clothes because we would be wearing cammos (camouflage uniforms) most of the time, so packing is no big whoop. At the last minute, I decide to bring Carlos my teddy bear for good luck, but that's about it for extras. Everything else will be taken care of is what the producers told us.

This show will air on Channel 46 at first, which is mostly reruns or Chinese news right now, but still. Channel 46 also shows the first couple seasons of *Standing Room Only*, which is my favorite '80s show. Mostly, I like how there is a girl with Down Syndrome and she is so funny. Her catch phrase is "Where's The Beef?" which was originally on a commercial, but the way she says it really cracks me up.

Mom and Dad and I have coffee in the morning and Dad wants to make his famous pancakes, but I say no way 'cause it will take too much time. Then when we're sitting at the kitchen table, they give me $100 and a brand new cell phone. Even though I don't really get it cause all my food is free and I think there's phones on the base, I say thanks. Then I say, Come On 'cause I don't want to miss the bus.

When we got to the meeting point in front of Pik'n'Pak at the Country Gate Mall, the cameras are rolling and I find out we're already on the show. A drill sergeant comes up and yells at me to get my name tag and find my group. I run up to a big table with stickers on it and find mine immediately. A lady with a headset tells me to fall in formation with Company E.

"Who are the LOSERS?" the drill sergeant keeps saying. "Which one of you is a PUSSY?"

A big crowd has formed on the other side of the parking lot. I see my parents standing with a bunch of other people behind a rope while photographers run around taking pictures. Even Carmela Cook, the famous traffic reporter, is here.

"Sergeant Burger smells some flab!" he says. "Let me try to sniff it out!"

I keep staring straight ahead, but can see him walking up and down the lines of all five teams. Sometimes he'll put his face right in somebody else's face and yell, "Boo!" or "Pantywaist!"

A couple teenagers from the parking lot shout, "You suck!" but he ignores them because he is an actor.

When he comes down my row, I stand still as a statue. There is no reason to be scared because Georgie warned us there would be lots of yelling and that we should stay tough.

After Sergeant Burger walks down all the rows, he goes to the front and says, "Atten-HUP! Listen up!" he says. "There's a lot of flab and a lot of frosting in this group and I'm not going to tolerate it. This is *Maneuvers*! You may have noticed, unless you are an idiot and can't count, that there are eleven troops in each unit. Eleven! What kind of number is eleven?"

I know from elementary school math that it is a prime number, but I don't say anything.

"It's one more than ten, that's what," he says. "Ten is what we need!"

This is when people start shuffling around and making some noises and he yells at us to be quiet. A lady watching from the parking lot screams out, "Don't be such a jerk to our loved ones!" and some guy in the line next to me says, "Oh shut up, Gloria!"

Then Sergeant Burger blows a whistle and tells everybody to drop and give him twenty. I whip through the first ten without a problem, but the next ten are pretty hard. At least I'm not the last one to finish. I hear my parents cheering me on.

"One of you has got to go! One from each group!" Sergeant Burger is yelling.

I am trying to have a positive attitude, but mostly I can tell it's going to be me. Always in my life I am the one that gets dropped, like in sports or choir or pep squad tryouts.

The cameras are going up and down the lines, getting a look at everybody. Rex Douglas the announcer is saying, "It's time to get this show on the road. Winners are born not made. It might not sound fair, but face it, life's not fair."

"We will give you one minute," the Sergeant says. "One full minute to fall out of line and take a good look at the troops in your squad. Looks may be deceiving, but so is life in general in these times. Listen carefully. Each group will be handed a grenade. When I blow my whistle, you will have one full minute to toss the grenade to the person you deem unfit for service."

He blows the whistle and right off the bat, the grenade gets tossed to me. I throw it to the woman on my right. She tosses it back to me.

All the while cameras are moving in and out, getting in our faces and Sergeant Burger is saying, "Who looks like they're gonna weigh you down when push comes to shove!?"

The grenade gets tossed back to me and I toss it back to the big guy who threw it at me in the beginning.

"Choose wisely!" he keeps saying. "Get rid of that hot potato!"

The grenade gets tossed at me again. I accidentally drop it and it rolls over to the boy next to me. He refuses to pick it up. Everyone is staring at me, yelling, "Pick it up, Morrison!"

I know I have time left, so I scurry over and pick it up and hand it to the guy who wouldn't grab it. He refuses to take it. "Take it, " I'm saying. "You have to take it!"

Then the whistle blows and I'm down there on the ground, still holding the grenade. Everyone starts clapping and going, "Woo! Yeah!" and stuff.

"Okay, flab! You're out! Meet at the picnic table to pick up your consolation prize."

I start walking over to the table when a photographer corrals me with the other losers.

"Hey! Let's get a picture of you all together," she says. "All you good sports."

I would be lying if I said I wasn't a little sad, but at least I got a chance. I got a lot further than some of the people who wanted to be on the show. The next day our picture was on the front of the Living section with a headline that said Flab Five. Mom wanted to cut it out and put it on the refrigerator, but I asked her not to.

Punchlining

Please know that I am not professionally trained in the art of mime. Though I have done much research about the origins and history of the celebrated form, I am the first to admit that I barely know what I'm doing out here. The makeup and leotard probably have you believing otherwise, but really it's just an illusion. And we all know what the Greeks said about illusions, right? Listen. I have consulted with some masters via email, done a little limbering up, and now it's time to hit the streets. Let's make it happen, people. As a performance artist and truth machine, the time is now.

Who can pinpoint when mimes became a big joke? My inner barometer places it sometime in the early '80s, but it's a question I've come back to over and again while studying at the Art Institute and preparing for this day. I walk out of my house, fully suited up, and stop at a sidewalk vendor in front of Radio Shack to buy a bacon-wrapped hot dog (Tijuana style). As the young girl rotates the double-meat treat on the greasy plank of sheet metal, I close my eyes and meditate on the answer. A low tremulous hum fills my ears and as the hum evolves into crashes of rumbling surf, there are flashes in my mind that help me. I see Vaudeville. Olde tyme skits. Prohibition. A family gathered 'round a radio. Plastic popsicle molds. A sock hop. Teenage porn stars. People begin dressing more comfortably, especially for air travel. Rainbow suspenders. Video games. Wolfgang Puck. And I think we've arrived: Death of the Mime/ Mime as Punchline.

At first, I thought maybe the solution was staging a workshop in La Mime at my warehouse space. I hold openings and performances on the weekends and we usually get a pretty good crowd of students, neighborhood people and even some downtown gallery owners who are trying to stay on top of the avant garde and freak scenes. If people actually tried learning the craft for a few hours and could see how difficult it was, maybe they wouldn't laugh so easily the next time someone on a late night talk show jokes about being chased by "angry mimes" or a character in a movie says, "Dude, things could be worse. She could have left you for a mime." Making fun of mimes has become as easy as making fun of erectile dysfunction or mullets, neither of which are laughing matters when it really comes down to it.

Last year I cut my hair into a mullet and wore a mustache for my final performance piece. In one day I went from a shaggy bedhead and van dyke to total buttrock hesher. When I walked out to start my show - and a big raspberry to the art critic at the weekly paper who praised the physical transformation thinking it was my performance - I could hardly concentrate on executing the real thing. The crowd just wouldn't stop laughing because I, Jack Armstrong, semi-art star/provocateur looked ridiculous to them. They couldn't even quiet down enough for me to get to my folk song, the real crux of the piece. The song was about the Salvadoran family who got evicted from my building the week before.

Does that sound terrible to you? Imagine it. Seeing a white art school graduate singing a folk song about evicted Salvadorans? Does it make you cringe to think about it? And does your uneasy feeling become worse when I speak of the *pupusas gordas* and *sabor delicado* in *las comidas que ella me ha preparado*. Just wondering, just checking.

I had just written the song that morning, and coupled with the fact that I don't know how to play the guitar and my singing is much like that of a ten-year-old girl wearing headphones and rollerblading down the sidewalk as she prepares for her musical theater audition by belting out "Shoeless Joe from Hannibal, MO" from *Damn Yankees*, well, I think we all know what I was trying to get at with that performance. Obviously, the next logical step was mime.

As I head up the street, people are beginning to stare at me pretty hard. Like they've never seen a mime eating a hot dog before. Whatever. I've borrowed these stretchy black pants from my roommate and they're starting to chafe already, but as we say, On With The Show. I turn a corner and *schink*! something hits me in the head. I turn around to find a dirty teenage couple slumped down in a doorway, laughing at me in slo-mo. Throwing their heads back and letting their mouths hang open.

Mental note: Ridicule of mimes has reached all social and economic echelons. I almost yell out to them, but respecting my role, I keep mum and decide to saunter over in kind of a Chaplin-like walk. More specifically, like Robert Downey Jr. playing Chaplin, which was extremely close, but full of its own distinct signifiers.

"Oh, shit," the girl says, thumping the back of her hand into her boyfriend's chest. "The clown is coming to get us."

Aha! They assume I'm a clown. Duly noted. I hover over the

couple, darkening them with my shadow and begin my first attempt at a routine.

"Listen, chief," the boy says, his head poking out of a navy blue hoodie. "Don't. Just don't."

I turn my pockets inside out and frown deeply, pushing my lips into an exaggerated pout. Admittedly, it's a cliché move, but I needed to establish communication and, as I said, I don't pretend to be a professional. I hold up my index finger as if to say, "One moment."

The girl sighs loudly, turning her cheek to me and says, "Shit."

I refuse to be deterred so quickly. Plus they don't seem to be in a rush to get anywhere soon and I need practice before I hook up with Jerry at the corner. I spring into action, becoming a child at play. Skipping an imaginary rope and puckering my lips as if whistling being careful not to make a sound. I mime sitting at a school desk, raising my hand as if to eagerly say, "Pick me! I have the answer!"

The couple keeps their gaze fixed, and the girl even stops scratching for second.

Ever so slowly, I lower my arm. Glacially, deliberately, lower and lower. My expression changes from bright-eyed wonder to an inaccessible blank stare.

Passersby have stopped. Off to the right, I hear an old man's voice say, "What's the occasion? Is it somebody's birthday?" Somebody else yells, "Go back to the Wharf! We don't want you in our neighborhood!"

The couple seems rapt with my performance. What would I do next? I roll up my pant leg and madly slap at my calf for a vein.

This was either a flash of genius, or perhaps a callow, embarrassing attempt at public service that made me glad I was in disguise. A voice in the back wonders aloud if I shave my legs, but I ignore them, busying myself with "cooking" my "tar" and "loading" my "works". I fear I've drawn the syringe too big in proportion to the imaginary spoon on my canvas of air, but I keep going, releasing the sweet serum into my bloodstream. I nod a few times and lay back on the sidewalk. I shut my eyes in the last dance of death. Applause.

Suddenly, I realize that my head is wet. I've o.d.'ed in a sticky puddle of some sort. I jump to my feet and without bothering to take a bow, sprint away, adrenaline surging through my body. Someone throws a beer can.

At the corner I find Jerry standing in front of the crepe place with the video camera like we planned. If only he had captured my maiden voyage.

"You look amazing!" he says, doing a lap around me. And then, "What's all this shit in your hair?"

"It was incredible!" I say, but then start to see stars, so I squat down for a second.

"Shhh!" Jerry hisses. "You're a mime, remember? No talking."

I stand back up and run my palm down the back of my head. It's all gooey and there's a couple hard things stuck in there. I didn't even know they sold candy corns in April.

A lady eating brunch on the patio behind us stands up and starts tapping Jerry on the shoulder. "Excuse me, gentlemen? You're blocking our view of the sidewalk?"

Jerry needed little provoking. "Oh, god, lady. Sorry!" he goes. "You're trying to peoplewatch and there are people in your way! I guess we're ruining your al fresco dining experience." His gigantic blue eyes were going like searchlights. "Hey! What else is on the agenda after your crepe? A little window shopping and then back to the rank hell cage of your terrifying existence because you're an empty soulless vacuum who just wants to be accepted?"

"Whoa, Jerry. Back off," I say.

The lady goes back to her seat, and I lean over towards her

making an exaggerated whoopsie face and say, "Sorry about that."

A guy at her table wearing sunglasses and a baseball hat advertising the latest Steven Soderburgh film leans back in his chair and snorts, "Shut up, mime." The table gets a big laugh out of this. Of course.

I pull two fingers across my lips like I was sealing a Ziploc bag and bow my head. I do love the way mimes are playful but have dignity. Unfortunately, Jerry hadn't caught this interaction on tape either.

"Let's head across the street and catch people going into the theater," he says. "It's an Eisenstein film. Probably pretty ripe."

I ham it up while dodging traffic and a couple of people honk. The way Jerry keeps yelling, "Watch out: Mime crossing!" and "You don't want mime blood on your hands!" I can tell he's not really in tune with my vision. He gets the camera ready as I spot a senior citizen lesbian couple at the box office buying tickets for the next show. While the cashier counts their change, I watch them kiss and then walk away holding hands. Here was my window. I pounce in front of them and draw the outline of a big heart on my chest. They seem mildly amused and, surprisingly, wait for more. I make the heart begin to pulse, beating strongly and growing bigger. My motions get quicker. The heart becomes the size of my armspan, it can't get any bigger. I raise my eyebrows in what I hope they interpret as an expression of sheer delight and then, I blank. I can't figure out what else to do, so I leap in the air and come down on one knee, throw in some jazz hands and pray they will take this as Curtain. But they just stand there staring at me and nodding. I clear my throat until the short one says, "Hey, guy. You got a hat or anything? I'll give you a buck."

"Don't give him a dollar," the other one says. "You owe me a dollar. You got a dollar, you give it to me!" They laugh and walk inside the theater.

Jerry is bored already. He wants me to offend people or at least bite it once or twice, but I've already explained to him that this isn't *America's Funniest Home Videos*. (Though I do have a great concept for something called *America's Funniest Homeless Videos* where homeless people do relay type races.)

"Let's get a beer," he says. "This got lame a lot faster than I thought it would."

I don't argue. I'm not like a lot of artists who won't admit when their concept stinks. Plus my balls were getting really mismanaged in those pantaloons anyway. We're at the corner and while we're waiting for the light to change, I look down and there's this woman slumped on the curb with her head shoved into her knees. Brown hair with some pink and white stripes. Neopolitan. The light changes and everybody starts moving except me. I tell Jerry I'll catch up with him in a second.

The girl's got her one of her arms extended, a swarm of bumblebees tattooed on her bicep, and between her fingers is an unlit cigarette. I reach for my lighter, a real, physical lighter not a pretend lighter, and squat down beside her, flicking it a few times until she finally lifts her head up and just says, "How?" Not What, but How. She's pretty trashed, all bloated and raw like she's been crying for a few days. Maybe crashing from speed. I motion to the cigarette in her hand and flick some more, but she doesn't move. I even do little puffing gestures and blow some imaginary smoke rings. Nothing. She just stares, blinking away like she doesn't understand English.

"Do you need a light?" I ask her.

Her lower lip trembling, she whispers. "I thought mimes weren't supposed to talk."

"I'm not a real mime," I say. "It's an experiment. A performance piece."

She looks at me for a second and then her face just falls. She lets out this huge moan. "Oh, god," she says, covering her mouth. "Oh, god. Oh, god! No!" Her stringy hair flies back as she bolts up and starts running toward a limousine parked in the median. The cigarette rolls into the gutter and is immediately retrieved by a pigeon. I lean over and offer it a light.

A Skill You'll Develop

When the time came to visualize our boxes, I pictured mine
like a treasure chest in a pirate movie. A chest washed up on the
shores of a deserted beach at sunrise. As soon as I was prompted by
the guide, I walked across a sea of clouds to open my box and a
golden ray shot out. I took a few steps back and when my eyes
adjusted, I saw on the end of the ray, just a few inches before my
nose, a scalloped halfshell like the kind goddesses are sometimes
cavorting on. The halfshell was sending me a sign. Right on top of it
sat the word Chi, in a sort of spiritual font, except I was seeing
double, so it was Chi Chi. And that's the story of how I found the
name for my business. Or rather, how the name found me.

I was telling this to the chick who wandered up to me at the
beach and asked to give my sticks a try. My Chi Chi Sticks. If you've

never had the opportunity to play with the sticks, you might think they're some flaky hippie thing. You would be sorely mistaken. I'm not in the habit of foisting my opinions on other people, I learned that lesson a long time ago, but if you think my sticks are interchangeable with hackeysack, I won't bother releasing the energy to contradict you. You are wrong and that is final.

To achieve any kind of chops on the sticks you have to develop a daily practice. I started with regular devil sticks, the kind where one stick is held in each hand and a third is flipped about with them. They're amusing enough, but after mastering them in less than a week, I needed to move on. I needed to be challenged again.

On a warm fall day, when I was feeling very clear from completing a week long juice fast, I whittled my own prototypes out of bamboo. Devil sticks were way too heavy, physically and spiritually. My prototypes had one handheld guiding stick and another with four small rubber cones, two on each end and two in the middle. The cones really brought it to a new level in regards to balance and strategy. With four areas of play instead of just one, the variations on stick juggling are limitless. The player doesn't experience the energy sink associated with the emotional claustrophobia of devil sticks.

As far as the business angle, the secret to my success is bringing my sticks with me everywhere I go. That's everywhere. The beach, concerts, street festivals. I'll whip them out while waiting for BART and sometimes get a few tips from passing commuters. I like to think of it as having three new appendages. Business started word-of-mouth, but now I sell Chi Chis to people all over the world via the internet. They are especially big in Germany after this jam band called Wunderad had me make special Wunderad sticks for their merchandise table. When you go to one of their concerts, they've got CDs, T-shirts, baseball hats and Chi Chi Sticks. I love it. And, what can I say? They're not too bad for meeting girls either.

"Ooh. Let me try," the girl at the beach had said. "Those really are different from devil sticks."

I took one look at her long auburn curls and the Aztec sun tattoo encircling her belly button and handed them over.

"Happy Solstice!" she said. The solstice was last week, but I didn't say anything. It's really the thought that counts.

Now naturally, someone who has mastered devil sticks is an ideal candidate to take on Chi Chis, and this girl was doing pretty well. A few surfers stopped to check her out, but I'm sure it wasn't just her technique they were ogling. She was wearing a very revealing crocheted tube top and a long white skirt with the hem tied up in a knot. Without glancing over, I could feel the surfers eyeing me, too. I knew what they were thinking. Another big, bearded, aging hippie with a thinning gray ponytail moving in on an innocent. Fascinating that some people must still feel the need to stereotype. I guess most surfers aren't too bright anyway.

"Wow," she said, handing them back over. "What's your name?"

"Leif," I said. "What's yours?"

"Not telling," she said. "Let's go swimming."

She slid down her skirt, revealing, as I had guessed, that she wasn't wearing any underwear. Oh, these girls. You know, I've been going after the same free spirit types for most of my life and I never get tired of them. Vibrant, energetic, flexible. I don't meet as many as I used to, but I have a theory on that. A part of it certainly has to do with me getting older and a bit less attractive, but really I just think kids today are changing. They're more jaded, more suspicious. Hooking up with a girl used to be a breeze, but now people aren't as trusting as they used to be. I find that very few girls nowadays, even in San Francisco, are open to living a free and open life. Exploring all the possibilities and relishing in life's magic.

I haven't always been this enlightened. Far from it. In my younger days, I may have taken a woman for granted once or twice. Feelings may have been hurt along the rows that were hoed because I always had my eye out for the next peach falling off the tree. Not anymore, Bub. The fact that an attractive young woman would still approach me on the beach was mindblowing. A fantasy. I wanted to make sure she knew how much I appreciated her positive approach. I wanted to be fun for her.

"Last one in's a rotten egg!" I yelled and ran into the surf.

"Eww!" she screamed, the little nymph. "I'm vegan!"

The swim was completely mystical. She was a fearless swimmer and followed me about a quarter mile out. We were treading water, looking out to the bridge on the horizon, when she turned to me and smiled. It was such a crooked, sexy little smile that I wanted to let out a soul-scrubbing primal scream. So I did. As we began the swim back in, three sea lions came up and swam right next to us. I tried to reach out and touch one, but the girl cried out, "Don't invade their space!" It was like they were challenging us to race them. They would swim ahead and then turn back and circle us. This had happened only a few times before in my life, and I took it as a sign that this girl was really something special.

We ran up on some rocks, sat in silence and watched the sun set. She was such a pretty girl, on the shorter side and nicely rounded. A real earth mother type. Her breasts were large and pendulous and I guessed that she'd probably never worn a bra in her life. Definitely not as common as it used to be.

"Where did you grow up?" I ventured. "Were your parents on a commune?"

"Hey!" she said. "Are you totally starving? I'm completely famished. Let's go to that place, Naked."

Naked was a raw food restaurant in the Avenues that seemed

really overpriced to me. If I have the money, I don't mind shelling out for expensive food that's prepared nicely, but this place seemed snobby. It was part of the new school health food invasion. I'd eaten there before with another girl, a trust fund kid, who paid for everything and let me take her home afterwards.

"Why don't we go to Mike's?" I said. "Better food at half the price. The staff is friendly, too."

"I want to go to Naked!" she said, sounding like a child. "I've never been. Oh, please. My treat!"

As I said before, I make my living from Chi Chi, and it had been a slow month. I guess if she was footing the bill.

"Okay," I said. "But I don't think we can go with the clothes we have on."

"Sure we can," she said. "Fuck 'em."

I pulled on my shorts and T-shirt and strapped on my sandals. As we walked back to my bus, she reached out and grabbed my hand. My good karma was coming back to me tenfold.

Finding parking in this neighborhood was always a bitch and I was getting a little stressed out. She wasn't talking much, just singing along to the radio, sighing every once in awhile when a potential spot turned out to be too small or in a towaway zone. We kept circling around the neighborhood and finally I said, "You know, Mike's has a lot we could park in."

"Leif," she said, fiddling with the feathers on my dashboard, "we're going to Naked. Just park anywhere. If you get a ticket, I'll pay for it. I promise."

I stepped on the brake and looked over at her intently. "You promise?"

"Totally," she said.

I pulled up onto the sidewalk behind a couple of other cars that had done the same thing and got out. She stayed sitting in the car until I realized she wanted me to come around and open the door for her. I hadn't opened the door for a woman since my high school prom. She was a bit of a puzzle, but I have to admit it was exciting. I hadn't been laid in months.

We walked into the restaurant and I immediately remembered everything I didn't like about it. It was one of those noisy, industrial spaces with lots of stainless steel. Very cold and sterile. Some kind of loud techno music was being pumped in and the concrete floors and high ceilings made every scrape of a plate earsplitting.

"Cool," the girl said. "Look at their outfits."

The staff uniform consisted of some form-fitting silver pants that looked like they didn't breathe at all and black T-shirts with the name of the restaurant spelled out in rhinestones on the front.

After a few minutes, the maitre d' approached us and asked if we had a reservation. It was still early and the place wasn't half full yet.

"Yes, we do," the girl said. "It's under Leif."

The maitre d' scanned his book before saying, "I'm sorry. I don't have anything here. Could it be another name? What's the last name?"

The girl glanced over at me and looked him right in the eye and said, "Tree. Leif Tree. Party of two."

The man stifled a laugh and pretended to look over the list of names again.

"No, I'm very sorry. There's no reservation listed under Leif or Tree."

The girl burst out with a big, hearty laugh. "I'm sorry, " she said. "I was totally lying!" She squeezed my hand. "It was worth a try, though."

To my surprise, he seemed a bit charmed by her and said, "Let me see what I can do."

A few minutes later he came back from the dining room and, with a completely straight face, said, "Yes. Tree? I can seat you now."

As we started walking towards him, he suddenly put the menus up over his mouth. "Excuse me, miss," he said. "We do ask that our customers wear some type of footgear."

I looked down at the girl's sandy toes and flinched.

"Really?" she said flirtatiously. "Oh, if I must then." She opened her bag and slid on a pair of flip-flops. "There," she said. "How's that?"

"That's just fabulous," the man said. "This way."

Once we were seated, I relaxed a little. The room was fairly dark and the girl looked even more gorgeous by candlelight. Everything sun-kissed and outdoorsy about her before had transformed into this aura of mystery and glamour. Even the sand in her eyebrows seemed to sparkle.

I ordered a tuber and pine nut "cheese" empanada and she got one of the specialty pizzas that feature buckwheat crusts "baked by the sun." She also ordered one of the most expensive wines on the menu. I balked at first when she said she wanted the $275 organic Pinot Noir, but it was her money. Who was I to argue?

After we got the ordering out of the way, I grabbed her hands in mine and said, "You are an angel. An absolute living, breathing angel who has come into my life today to spread some of your blessed joy."

She said, "Let's play a game. It'll keep our minds off our stomachs until the food gets here."

"Okay," I said. She was as playful as the trickster in Native American storytelling.

"I'll say a word and you say what pops into your mind."

"Ah. First thought, best thought," I said. "I'm game."

She said, "Love."

I said, "Hate."

She said, "Ashbury."

I said, "Poet."

"What?" she said.

"The poet John Ashbery," I said.

"Oh," she said.

"Go on," I said. "Poet"

"Words," she said.

"Sentence," I said.

"Prison."

"Bars."

"Windows."

"Doors."

"Jim Morrison."

"Nice," I said. "Um, Dead."

"Old."

"Young."

"Child."

"Porn."

"What?" she said.

I was mortified. How did that come out of my mouth? Why did I say Porn when she said Child? She was looking at me with her mouth wide open.

"Why did you say that?" she said. "That is so gross."

"No, no!" I said. "Believe me, I have no idea why that came out of my mouth. I'm sorry. That was very offensive. I, I just must have been reading about the case out in Concord in the newspaper."

The lights in the restaurant flickered and then went out.

"Just a rolling blackout," a waiter announced. "Nobody panic. We'll get more candles." We'd been having these blackouts for weeks.

"I'm going to go to the bathroom," the girl said, pushing her chair back from the table.

While she was gone, I decided to try to defend myself better when she came back. It was just a stupid game. It didn't mean anything. It's harmless word association. When a person is able to free their mind, and a lot of people can never even get to that point, things like this are bound to happen sometimes. It goes with the territory of exploration and self-discovery. That terrible story has been in the news every day for the past month and I'm sure it infiltrated my unconscious mind. It's a perfectly natural occurrence.

Our waiter came by and put another candle on our table.

"Sorry about this, sir," he said, opening our bottle of wine. He put his face in close to mine and whispered, "Let me know if you need anything else." He filled the glasses and I swear it looked like he gave me a little wink when he walked away.

What kinds of pheromones was I giving off that had all these good-looking kids flirting with me? Not that I was into men, per se, but I'd had my youthful dalliances and a few group encounters at The Grange. That was the early '70s, though. I'd stuck with women ever since, but it didn't bother me if a man was attracted to me. I didn't have any hang-ups.

The girl came back a few minutes later and tasted her wine before speaking. "I'm sorry I got upset, Leif. It just seemed gross, that's all."

"I know, " I said. "I'm sorry. It just came out. I was allowing myself to think outside the box. I'm not a bad man. "

"I know you're not, " she said. "Let's have a toast."

Relieved, I held up my glass and said, "To the beginning of a wonderful friendship."

"Peace out," she said.

After our food arrived, we didn't talk much. There were so many things I wanted to ask her. Where she was from. What her passions were. Her name.

The lights came back on and the girl started looking around the restaurant. She seemed distracted. I wished she was staring as intently into my eyes as I was into hers, but I appreciated her young person's curiosity about new surroundings.

"My pine nut cheese is very delicious," I said. "Would you like to try it?"

"Oh, no thank you," she said. "Would you like a pattypan squash?"

I don't enjoy squash much, but didn't want to pass up her offer. She was reaching out to me, literally, with her fork.

"I hate these things," she said. "Too bitter!"

I grabbed the hand she had the fork in and said, "My god, that's exactly how I feel."

She made a face. "Well, why did you say you wanted it then?"

"What?" I said.

"If you think they're too bitter, why did you say you wanted to eat it?"

The lights went back off and I took it as an opportunity to reevaluate my whole performance on this date. Why was I acting this way? Acting desperate. That word association game had really thrown me off-kilter.

"I think I have some water in my ear," she said. "I'm going to go to the ladies' room and hop up and down on one leg for awhile."

I waited for her for a long time. Too long, really. At some point, my intuition told me that she had left and I wandered back to the bathrooms to double check. It felt terrible waiting outside the ladies' room so I could ask the woman walking out if she was inside. She looked at me like I was some kind of creep, some kind of old pervert who lurks outside women's restrooms on a regular basis. But I can't worry about petty judgments. She'll get hers.

What was I going to do now? The bill was probably somewhere in the range of four hundred dollars. I didn't have that kind of money and I certainly didn't have any credit cards.

With the power out, I knew I could probably get away with sneaking out, but then I would have to face the karmic retribution later. How bad would it bite me for ditching the check at an overpriced restaurant that was already making a killing by exploiting the organic food craze? Then again, maybe this was my instant good karma. I was done wrong by someone I trusted, so now I get a free dinner out of it. Did that make sense? One thing was sure. I couldn't just sneak out the back door because my satchel was still sitting on the floor by the table. It only held my beach towel and my prototypes, but those sticks were good luck. They were definitely positive forces. I could grab the bag and head right for the exit without turning back. If anyone caught me, I'd say I needed something from my bus. Oh, shit. The bus. I'm sure I'd gotten a ticket by now. Maybe I'd even gotten towed. That's what I will get in return for not paying the bill. That will be my punishment. My car will be gone once I get outside. Should I go outside and see if the car is okay before I sneak out for good? I felt paralyzed, standing there outside the ladies' room, watching these women give me the evil eye.

I went into the men's room to think. There were scented candles all around that smelled like rosemary and myrrh. Quite soothing, actually. I went into one of the stalls, closed the door and sat down. Then it occurred to me. I had enough money in my fannypack for a tip. Maybe if I left a tip for the waiter, my payback would be less harsh. Perhaps when I went outside, I would only have a ticket instead of being towed. That made sense. I would go back to the table, grab my satchel and leave a tip on the table.

Suddenly, the lights went back on. The techno started up. Damn it. Was this some sort of sign? Were the gods telling me I needed to face the music? I got up and splashed my face with cold water just as the waiter came in. "There you are," he said. "I thought you two ran out on me."

I doubled over, clutched my stomach and started groaning.

"Are you okay, sir?"

"Oh, lamb," I said. "This is embarrassing, but I feel very, very sick."

He ran over and put his hand on my shoulder. "Would you like to sit down, sir? Can I get you a glass of water? A cool washcloth?"

I let my knees buckle and hit the floor. "A washcloth," I said. "That would be nice."

He hurried for the door and as soon as he was gone, I stood up and went for the back exit, leaving my lucky sticks behind. I ran through the back courtyard and around the corner to where I'd parked. The bus was still there. No ticket either. I unlocked the door and wondered when it would all come down.

What's Up There

Tony rested his forehead on the steering wheel and banged it lightly a couple times. The back of his neck looked like a pack of franks. "Why?" he asked. "Why us?"

It was Saturday morning and everybody was lined up trying to get into the parking lot at the big warehouse food emporium.

"Because this is when people like us come here," I answered, even though I didn't think he was looking for an answer.

Tony looked offended. "What do you mean by 'people like us'? What are we? Who are we, Marcia?"

My mother was right. Tony was turning into a cranky old man. "Honey, when people work during the weekdays, they do their shopping on the weekends. That's how it goes. That's how it's always been." I put my palm on top of his bald spot and gave it a couple pats. "It's okay. We're almost in."

Tony manages a furnace and air conditioning place in Glendale where we've lived for almost thirty years. The closer he gets to retirement, the more antsy he's getting. The more impatient with everything. He's a walking heart attack, our daughter Charise keeps saying. Type A, she says. He needs mugwort and milk thistle or something like that. She's up in San Francisco studying Chinese medicine, at least I hope she's studying and not working in that bar anymore. The last time she visited she spent a long time poring over her dad's tongue. All those bumps and colors mean things. She also said she could tell by looking at his face, where the wrinkles were and the shadows, that he had a damp spleen. I'm not sure what that is supposed to mean exactly because I would normally consider any internal organ to be sort of damp, wouldn't you?

"As long as she's happy and she doesn't get mixed up with drugs," Tony says. "She never asks for money and that's something these days."

Tony's always been funny about drugs. When we first met, we were kids. In our teens and everybody was smoking grass. Not Tony, though. He was just a drinker. Like a man on one of those shows from the '50s. He liked his Manhattans or a scotch on the rocks. And beer, of course. We'd all be at the beach, kind of fuzzy and playing music, and he'd always show up with a case of beer and carton of True Blue Filter Kings tucked under his arm. I loved the way he looked. Real sturdy. He'd plop down on the blanket and we'd smoke a whole bunch of those cigarettes and take turns playing the guitar. We finally quit smoking in '97 even though I still want one almost every afternoon when I get off my shift at the hospital.

"Oh, get a load of this guy," Tony says. "How does that grab you?" One of those big SUVs was trying to get around us and steal our parking space.

"That thing looks like a tank," Tony says. "Nice tank!" he yells out the window while trying to maneuver the Civic around them. Tony kept inching up and the guy next to us kept inching up and pretty soon our cars were almost touching.

Then Tony starts laying on the horn. God, I hate it when he gets all sweaty. He was nervous. He just turned fifty and all of a sudden he got more nervous. Even driving places we'd been going together forever. It made me sad to think of him getting old and jumpy. He shakes his fist out the window like some Italian in a movie. I'd never seen him do that before. How could someone pick up a new gesture at fifty?

We circled around the lot a few times, and almost had a spot, but some kid whipped in before Tony could react. He was lining the car up just right and this kid in some red jobber swoops in on the spot.

"I should call the cops!" Tony shouts, even though he hates the cops. Before I realize it, he's jumped out of the car and is knocking on the kid's window. "Come out of there, you ape! You saw me waiting. You knew we wanted that spot! Do you think I'm just going to go away? Disappear? Do you?"

People behind us started honking. People who had bought their things and were ready to leave were trapped in here. "Please, Tony!" I was yelling through the window.

I see the kid take a deep breath and open his door. It was like a bad comedy the way this kid steps out of his little hot rod and was a full foot taller than Tony. And he's wearing a red tank top. It matched the car! And his body was heavily oiled. Shiny. Like a wrestler or a bodybuilder or who else gets all oiled up? Like that Richard Simmons when he goes on a talk show. Now here's the weirdest part. He, I'm not kidding, slaps Tony across the face. This big guy who could have packed a manly punch, just slaps him across the face like a woman would.

Not me, I mean. I've only slapped Tony once a long time ago back when we were first dating. Gosh, it was dumb. He was working for the electric company and I was only doing part-time down at Coco's while I was in nursing school. He came in and I knew he'd been out with some other woman. I could smell perfume. It was just Joanne from work, he said. He had to wait awhile before this one job, so they had a couple over at the Hotsy. And I just didn't think for a second and slapped him. Everybody at the counter stopped what they were doing and tried not to look at us. He walked out all mad, but we made up right when I got home. And that's all. I knew I didn't have anything to worry about with him anyway, but something else took over that night and I slapped him. Just like this kid did.

So I open the door and step one leg outside and leaned over the top of the car. I'm yelling for him to get back in the car and then Tony tries to swing back at him. A punch. But the kid just grabs his wrist with one hand and that was the end of that. Tony knew it wasn't going to go anywhere and got back in fuming.

"That cracker slapped me! Did you see that? Just like a woman would. Maybe he was queer! A towel-snapper!"

The horns were really going now. A lady behind us started shouting, "Uh? Hello? Hel-lo?" She sounded like Charise, but when I turned around she was as old as me. And with a bad facelift. It's rude, I know, but that's my new thing. Spotting people my age who've had plastic surgery. It's interesting, that's all.

The weird thing was, the whole incident seemed to lighten Tony up actually. Getting slapped. When we finally found a space, he was still saying, "Like a woman! Slapping my face like that."

We walked into the store, arm in arm, laughing about it.

"Next we'll probably see him in the ladies' underwear aisle," Tony was saying. I laughed along, mostly because I wanted to keep him in good spirits.

"Or maybe pantyhose," I said.

"Yeah. That's it! Studying the pantyhose. What a fruit."

We were just about to get our handtruck when Tony says, "Hey! Don't those nachos smell good? Let's get a big plate of nachos first."

I got us a table and Tony came back with the plate and some napkins. It was so loaded down with cheese and jalapenos that the grease was already soaking through. "Look at this thing," he said. "This thing is like a walking heart attack."

It made us think of Charise. She hadn't been calling us much lately and I could tell Tony was a little worried. We'd left a few messages, but she wasn't calling us back. I think her school was on a mountain or something and maybe that was why. Maybe she couldn't get a signal for her cell phone. Maybe she had a new boyfriend.

So, all of a sudden I say, "Let's go up and see her. Let's go to San Francisco and visit our little girl."

"When?" Tony says, licking cheese from his fingers. "When do we have any time anymore?"

"I think we should go right now," I say. "Come on, Tone! Remember when we just took off and went to Vegas? Wasn't that fun?"

"Now?" Tony says. "Right now? You're crazy, lady. We can't just do that. We can't just leave town without any notice. She isn't expecting us. We can't just surprise her out of nowhere."

I push out my lower lip and make a pouty face and some kid eating beef jerky behind us sticks his tongue out at me. "That kid just stuck his tongue out at me!"

Tony whips around real fast and the kid ducks under the table. "Ha! Scared him," Tony says. "Anyway, we got that party for Frank's retirement tonight. I think they even hired hula dancers for out by the pool."

"Honey, you think Frank is a pompous ass. You didn't want to go anyway."

"But I've never been to San Francisco, Marcia. We can't just go now. What if we run into George?"

George is Tony's younger brother. For a long time after he got out of jail on those child pornography charges we didn't know where he was. Northern Cal somewhere, but then Charise ran into him up there in the city. Of course he didn't recognize her cause she's all grown up now, but she knew him right off from pictures. Turns out he was still being his sleazy old self and trying to pick up on her and her friends on Haight Street. Giving them some fake hippie name or something. That really did it for Tony.

"We're not going to run into George," I told him. "You can't never go to San Francisco because you're afraid of running into him."

Tony buries his face in his hands real dramatic.

"We could fly out of Burbank," I singsong. "It'll only take an hour."

He opens a few fingers to let one of his eyes peek out. He's always wanted to go to San Francisco and he knows it and I know it.

He starts picking at some melted cheese on the plate and eating it off his thumbnail. "What about clothes? What about our toothbrushes? By the time we get out of here and get our stuff."

"It's only ten. We can leave right now and try to meet Charise for an early dinner. We can come back late tonight. If she can't make it, she can't make it, but we can still go out to the wharf and get some fried seafood."

"Yeah," Tony says. "And we could get some of those steam beers."

Maybe we went back and forth a little more, but soon enough

we were walking right out of the food court and headed to the airport. I don't want to sound corny or like I read too many magazines, but we really needed to spice things up a little. Break out of our daily routines and have fun like we used to. We used to have a lot of fun.

Boy, I love small airports. They're so easy to get around and at Burbank when you get on the plane, you get to walk right out on the tarmac and feel just like a movie star boarding a private jet or something. Of course we weren't on a fancy jet, we were on one of those cheapie airlines where the flight attendants crack jokes the whole way. The smoking section is located out on the wing and our featured movie will be *Gone With The Wind* and all that. It was a riot. Tony thought they should take their jobs a little more seriously, considering our lives were in their hands and all, but I said lighten up. We need more humor in this crazy world. I mean, he was fine after a couple cocktails and by the time the pilot reached cruising altitude and announced he was going to put the thing on autopilot and come back and enjoy a drink with us, Tony was laughing right alongside everybody else.

Once we got off the airplane, we found a phone and called Charise. We got her machine and told her we'd check back, but I didn't say where we were. I didn't want her to feel bad.

The city was freezing. I couldn't believe we left a scorching hot day in Glendale and now we were sitting in all this fog. It felt like we were a million miles away. We hopped on a shuttle and just laughed and laughed at all the people lugging that baggage everywhere. It felt so free. We were holding hands and enjoying the sights the whole ride down to Pier 39.

First things first is that we stopped at a T-shirt stand and got some souvenir sweatshirts cause it was so darn cold. I got the '49ers and Tony got kind of a classy navy blue one with the Golden Gate

Bridge on it. Charise would die if she saw us looking like such tourists, but that I guess that's part of a kid's job. Making fun of your parents. Besides, we were tourists.

"This place is like an amusement park," Tony kept saying.

On our way to find a phone again, we came across this mime in front of the aquarium, and I hate to say it, but he wasn't really very good. I'm used to Shields & Yarnell. I know that street performers are a whole other breed and Robin Williams used to be one with Whoopi, but this kid had a long way to go. Anyway, we gave him a buck and went into an Irish pub to get a beer and try Charise.

No luck. This time I made sure to tell her how much we loved her and it wasn't her fault that her Mom and Dad were so crazy as to plan this whirlwind trip. I said, you know, that we'd be at that famous Italian seafood place on the Wharf for awhile and then we'd stop by that other famous place for Irish coffees and if she got the message and had time, she should try and meet us. Tony was rolling his eyes at me like I was saying too much, but of course then he had to get on the phone and go to town with all the mushy talk himself. I guess we were getting a little tipsy, but hey, we were on vacation.

After we royally pigged out on seafood and pasta and more beer and those Irish coffees, it was T minus three hours until our flight back to Burbank. I got a wild hair up my bottom and thought we should go to Chinatown. I'd been to the Chinatown in Los Angeles a few times, but this one was supposed to be the best.

"Tone, get us to Chinatown!" I said.

"Get thee to a nunnery, you strumpet!" That was the only Shakespeare Tony knew and he only broke it out when he was drunk.

But what a great navigator he was. He got us right in the middle of all the action in no time. We were stumbling around and laughing at all the weird smells. Tony was being bad and kept talking with this Chinese accent. I was trying to shush him, but he would point at one of those skinned birds in the windows and say, "Dee-rishus plessed dok."

He didn't get what was wrong with it. He said it's the same thing as me telling my Princess Diana jokes with a fake English accent, but I don't agree. This seemed different to me.

So we walked past this bar and Tony says, "Let's get one more for the road." It looked mostly like Chinese people and I didn't know if I wanted him in there being all rowdy, but he dragged me in.

I got the weirdest feeling when I walked in. Like we were interrupting or something. I'll give it to the bartender, though. She was friendly. I don't even know if she spoke English. Well, she must have, right? She had on a lot of makeup and a short skirt, but she smiled a lot.

Tony told me to get us some desserty drinks, something sweet like mai tais and went to go find the bathroom. And then it hit me that I didn't feel like going home. Why couldn't we get a motel and go back tomorrow? As soon as Tony finished some of his drink, I was going to bring it up.

So Tony was in the bathroom and I guess I was just sort of sitting there watching these older men playing dice on the bar when it happened. I had my back turned to the door and someone ran in real fast and put a paper bag in my lap. A lunch size paper bag. By the time I turned around, he was running out the front door again. I think he was a teenager by the way he moved. Now my gut instinct was to drop it on the floor. I didn't know what was in it, but I knew it wasn't meant for me. I also flashed back to this time in sixth grade when Lauren Pruitt, who was very popular, gave me a brown paper bag and said "Is this your lunch?" Well, when I looked inside it wasn't my lunch at all, just a bag full of dog poop. I was so embarrassed. The whole class was looking at me and laughing. I think they were all in on it together.

Tony finally came back and I wanted to let him sit down for a minute before I told him what happened, but then he tells me he thinks something funny is going on in the basement. I was kind of dizzy from all the drinks and my mind was racing about the bag. What if it was a gun? Or some kind of drugs? The music was so loud I didn't think I could tell him about it without yelling, so I pointed down and then tapped it with my foot.

This is the part where it gets really strange. Tony's looking at me like I'm nutters and then all the lights go out. Music, lights, everything. It's one of those rolling blackouts we've been hearing about on the news. Everybody in the bar starts yelling and making noise and Tony flips out. He grabs my arm and starts saying we have to leave. We have to get out of here. I probably shouldn't have done it, but I reached down and grabbed the bag. I also bonked my head on the bar.

Tony's hustling me out and I shove the bag inside my purse and don't say a word about it. It's not until he falls asleep on the way to airport that I look and see it's money. One thousand two hundred twelve dollars to be exact.

Of course I spent it. There were a few small things we needed for the house. A new can opener for one and some dish towels. When the coffeepot broke, I used that money for a replacement. I don't know what else. I honestly can't remember. A nice leather billfold was about fifty dollars. It's not like I could go out and buy a diamond ring and Tony wouldn't notice. I wasn't going to hide it from him. It just gradually dwindled down between groceries and haircuts and MiracleGro. I never told him anything. I never told anyone because when you stack it all up, everything considering, it wasn't much.

The Cool

I had parallel-parked the car with great difficulty and now I was just sitting there, actually kind of winded because the car doesn't have power steering. I used to be such a hot shit parallel parker. Hills, whatever, no problem. I knew it wasn't the car, it was me. No matter how much money I had or didn't have, I always kept the same beater. Mid-sixties MOPARs, man. Why drive anything else when these things look cool and keep on running. Loads of my shining qualities were waning by the hour, but the parallel parking one really hurt. It made me less tough. How could I possibly be getting less tough and more callous at the same time? I felt like the oldest mama lion in the zoo who keeps acting like she's feasting on fresh kill when she knows the trainer is actually cutting up the little chunks of meat for her.

I sat still listening for awhile. Sirens. Horns. Car alarms. Has someone sampled all of these and put them in a song yet? What am I thinking, of course they have. But maybe that was back in '86 which means it's about high time to add every imaginable ring on a cell phone and digitally remaster it. Maybe just an all-cell phone ring song. It deserves its own. With beats behind it. I sat there in the car thinking about shit like this, picking at the cracked plastic on the dashboard, until my watch clicked over to noon and my hands had stopped shaking. I went inside to get a drink.

All I was having was beer. A beer in the afternoon while I read my stack of papers and magazines. It was moronic how quickly I could get through the whole thing now. Like twenty magazines and eight papers in an hour. Same three-name wonderboobed actress on six of the magazines, regurgitating the same quotes about her relationship to the Catholic church and how her favorite food is chocolate doughnuts dipped in sour cream.

The bar's dark and smells musty, kind of like the Pirates of the Caribbean ride at Disneyland. It's been years since I've been here; this bar was never very popular, and happily, it looks like it still isn't. I suppose it's early still, but the doom is particularly overwhelming. Not doom in a sexy skid row or itinerant alcoholic way, just washed-up. Washed-up and not originating from a mighty or sparkling sea to begin with, but rather coming from a source that is stagnant and definitely non-potable. It really was the perfect place for me.

The only other customer was this incredible specimen of a late '80s Haight Street rocker. Long wavy hair, a little crusty on the ends from cheap mousse; motorcycle jacket with its surfeit of metal rings; ripped 501s folded up and in at the bottom so they're pegged on top of the well-worn Doc Martens. Docs with red laces even. One flannel on and one tied around his waist. A classic.

A few years ago this would have really made my day. I would

have gotten someone on the phone immediately and started shouting, "You will never guess in a million years what I'm looking at!" Whoever I called on the other end of the phone would be rattling off the usual obvious answers, names of game show hosts or child stars, until I finally gave in. After a good dramatic pause, acting as if I was really looking at the Hope Diamond or the first homo erectus, I'd say, "A real live grunge rocker."

The bartender rested her hand on my fingertips. "Can I take a look at this?"

She was holding up my copy of *Gem*. It almost looked like she was wearing fake blue contact lenses, which would be really unfortunate, but it was too dark to tell for sure.

"Yeah. You can have it," I said. "So, you're a big Ashley Tanya Lowell fan?"

"Oh yeah!" she said. "I love the way she is so dedicated to her craft. I also admire the range she showed in *Kissing Cousins III*."

This made the bartender seem pretty okay.

"Why do you have all this crap?" she said.

I considered making her feel bad for prying, but decided to come clean about most of it. "I need it all for my job. I mean, I don't have to pay for it. I write it off."

"Whoa. What kind of job lets you do that?"

She was like a baby. A freshly washed baby with pink skin, chubby cheeks and teeth like Chiclets. The only minor flaws on her face, the only thing giving it a semblance of texture at all, were the little holes from retired piercings in her chin and nose. I can't remember ever looking like that. New and vaguely elastic.

I pulled out a cigarette and she lit it for me.

"You remind me of Deborah Harry," she said. I looked up at her over the smoke. "That's totally a compliment," she added.

"I know," I said.

A cone of sunlight yawned through the room as a guy walked

in. Same guy. The rocker. I hadn't seen him leave, but when the girl nodded at him and he went straight to the bathroom, I figured it was probably a heroin thing.

She refilled his Guinness and walked back over to my side. "Do you have kids?"

"No," I said. And then to give her some shit, "Do you?"

She started laughing. "No way! I'm only 22. I guess I could have kids, but that'd be pretty sad if I had a baby and I was still working in a bar."

"It would?" I said. I really wished I hadn't started talking in the first place. I didn't give a shit about this stupid girl's life. And look at me, chitchatting with her like I needed company. Like I couldn't sit at a bar by myself without resorting to small talk.

"So, you have to tell me," she said. "What kind of work do you do so that you get to sit in bars and read magazines all day?"

The rocker came out of the bathroom and broke in. "Charise. You don't know who this is?"

She looked at him, back at me, back at him. "No. Should I?"

I turned to him. "You don't know me."

He held his palm up at me. The grunge rocker was doing "talk to the hand" at me. Now I almost got on the phone to call someone.

"Seriously, Charise?" he said to the bartender. "You don't know?"

"I mean, she looks famous or something. I told her that already."

"Well, maybe you're too young," he said.

"Shut up," Charise said.

I took a drag from my cigarette and put my head down on the bar.

"Charise, we are in the presence of one of San Francisco's most scandalous debutantes."

"Cool," she said, grinning. "Why are you so scandalous?"

I ignored her and rolled my head over toward the guy.

"You're Cricket Stoller, right?" he said.

I conceded. Fuck these people. "Yeah," I said. "Different last name now, but yeah."

He stood up and came a bit closer, looking into my face and then sat back down. "Can I tell her?" he asked.

I closed my eyes and waved him on with my cigarette. "Let her rip, Soundgarden." I looked at him again, wondering if I knew him, hoping I'd never slept with him.

"Oh, Cricket Stoller," he said. "Crick-et! They don't make them like you anymore. Now stop me if I'm wrong."

"I probably won't. Stop you, I mean." I kept thumbing through my magazines, listening.

"Cricket's father made his money in, what? Farming tools? Chicken feed? Something real downhome and wholesome."

I looked up, straight at my reflection in the mirror behind the bar. "Bovine hormone supplements," I offered. "Not so wholesome, really."

"Well, compared to those nasty DeHaros or the Palermos. God, the Palermos were full-on Mafia, weren't they?"

I put out my cigarette and stopped myself from reaching for another.

"Anyway, Cricket's mum is from England. The British Isles." He stated this in an overexaggerated Cockney accent for a second, a bad one, and then quickly stopped. "More than anything Mummy wanted little Cricket to be a proper girl. A deb right alongside the rest of the Pac Heights club. But Daddy was a little coarse, a farmer from the Midwest."

"He was a scientist," I added.

The bartender poured herself a shot of Jaeger and downed it.

"Cricket never fit in with the social set. Her white gloves were always dirty and her hair was often messed up."

I slid a cigarette out of the pack. The bartender took one for herself without asking.

"Hair is a woman's crowning glory," I said.

"What?" the girl laughed.

"That's a quote from my mom," I said.

"Awesome," the girl said.

"Didn't you even get a job at one point?" the rocker said. "During school?"

"Can you get me another?" I picked my glass up off the bar.

Charise held up her hand and wouldn't take my money.

"Yes, I embarrassed the family by getting a job at Cool Licks, the frozen yogurt shop. And later I worked at Zanzibar, this tacky clothing store on Polk."

"Pretty soon, you dropped out of Sacred Heart and were living with some old guy. A friend of Peter Joplin's dad." He stopped, looking extremely pleased with himself. "And then what?"

"Uh... and then I got really into drugs?" I suggested.

"Oh! Right! You got into drugs before you moved to New York. It was in New York that you had the complete meltdown."

I closed the magazine and caught myself doing an obviously fake yawn.

"Sorry," he said quickly. "But you did wind up in rehab and finally had to come back here and live at your parents' house again. Right?"

"That is right," I said flatly. "You are correct."

"Oh, wait, Charise," he said to the bartender. "I skipped all the fabulous parts. Cricket Stoller, the It Girl of 1985. Partying with all that New York trash. It must have given your mother a heart attack to see you photographed with all those models and fags and dirty old rock stars."

"Actually, she had a stroke," I said. "Dad had the heart attack."

Charise gasped and grabbed my arm. "Oh my god, I'm so sorry," she said and then turned to the guy. "Rick!"

Rick said, "Sorry."

I was lying about that part. My mom and dad were still relatively healthy, unhappily married and living in the same place on Jackson Street. I'd had breakfast with my dad that morning.

"And then," he said, "*People* magazine ran a story. Just one page, but with this incredible photo. Totally disturbing really. You looked like you weighed about eighty-six pounds. Do you remember?"

"Yep."

"You were...," he turned to Charise, "she was squatting down on a dance floor at some place in Manhattan. Completely crowded dance floor. And there's Little Miss Deb falling out of her clothes, slumped down against a wall."

"Oh no! You passed out?" Charise said. "I hate when that happens."

"Her eyes were open! For all I know, she was in something like a k-hole. Such a trendsetter. Were you doing tranquilizers or what?"

I shrugged my shoulders.

"It was creepy because your eyes were open, but you just looked so lost."

"Poor, poor me," I said.

"I'm sure all the society ladies had a field day with that one," he said. "My mother sure did."

Finally, a window. I sat up and looked directly at him for the first time. "Your mother?" I said it like I meant something by it. Amused. Like I knew all about her. And then I said it again. "Your mother? God, if you want to get me started on your mother."

It worked. He told me to fuck off and polished off the rest of his beer in silence. I swear sometimes I felt like I kept living just for tiny moments like this.

"So wait," Charise said. "Why the magazines? What are you doing now?"

I put my right elbow up on the bar to block off Rick, who was clearly dealing with some personal issue.

"Well," I told her. "It's ridiculous. More ridiculous than my party girl tour of duty. I figure out what is supposed to be cool and then I write up reports and sell them to whomever. Magazines. Stylists. Record companies. Shoe companies."

"No way!" she said. "That's a job? You get paid for that?"

"Charise. That's your name, right?" I said.

"Uh-huh."

I flipped open a magazine to an article about some young singer who hadn't even put out her first album yet.

"This girl," I said, "is no more or less cool than you."

She turned the magazine around to get a better look. "Well, I definitely don't like her pants." She rubbed a few fingers over the photo. "And I think it's stupid the way the pockets are ripped off and the threads are hanging all over the place."

"If I wanted to make you into a girl like this, not famous, just an up-and-comer with a photo spread, I could do that with a few phone calls."

"Really?" she said. "That's crazy."

"Exactly," I said.

"She's lying," Rick said, staring at his reflection. "She's a drug addict and a liar."

"Shut up, Rick. Look who's talking anyway," Charise said.

God, I hated these people. I really did.

The girl reached over the bar and punched him in the arm, then the face. Kind of near his eye. He flung his arm out and hit her on the side of the head. When the yelling started, it was typical drunk lovers shit. Fucking cunt. Loser. Asshole. I Hate You. Junkie.

Motherfucker. Etc. Not a creative insult from either of them. It made me want to lay down and take a nap, but I knew I should leave. I left my magazines and papers on the bar, got up off the stool slowly and walked out the door.

Charise was right on my heels. Once I was outside, she grabbed me by the arm, her baby face all red, fake blue eyes watering. Definitely fake now.

We squinted at each other for a second in the sun, and I said, "Look."

"I believe you," she said. "I could tell you really thought I was cool."

The entire weight of my head was being supported by two fingertips at the bridge of my nose.

"And if you care," she said, "I think you're cool, too." She put an ice cold hand on my arm and said, "I swear to God."

I can't remember if I spoke again. If I did, I said something stupid. All there was to do was walk back to the car and get inside.

Credit Card Test

It was an unusually temperate day on the Lower East Side of Manhattan as I carried my bagel and coffee, passed Hugh Grant on the street, climbed the stairs of my friend's fourth story walk-up and promptly shaved off my pubic hair. What was I thinking? Why didn't I just eat my breakfast and go to a museum like everybody else?

Instantly, I was horrified. Too scared to leave the house, thinking if I were struck down by a car or, more likely, that the shooting pain in my head was something serious, I would drop dead and my parents would be forced to identify the body. As the coroner ripped off the sheet with the flourish of a magician, my unpierced and tattoo-free body would be made to look all the more ridiculous with a razor-rashed pussy screaming out like a beacon of dashed hopes and clumsy technique.

Mom and Dad would want to get to the bottom of this one, so like Laura Palmer I would be subject to an investigation to uncover my secret life. But there would be no evidence of employment at strip bars, houses of prostitution, sex clubs, or performance art loft parties. No pasty-faced perverts would step forward to say that they were my special interest clients and all seventy-four of the people who have come in contact with my vagina would be tracked down and interviewed separately. Even that speedhead bike messenger who kicked me out after I made him pancakes on his birthday and all would uniformly respond that they remembered (fondly) a soft, silky downy lambchop and not the bald horror presented to them via these perfectly-focused Polaroids.

Lord in Heaven, bring us comfort as we face the excruciating details of what must have transpired in her final hours.

Nope, the report would say. It looks like Cricket Stoller was just on vacation. She woke up late, as usual. Purchased a bagel and a coffee, cream no sugar, saw Hugh Grant on the street, wasn't a fan, didn't think anything of it. She just shaved off her pubic hair. Badly. Apparently, the bagel was poppyseed.

My parents, hungry for answers, will watch the investigator pop another Rolaid into his pink mouth, hang his head in hamfist hands and say, "Welp, we determined your daughter didn't commit this act at the request of a sexual partner and she obviously couldn't make any money off that thing. It appears just to be poor, poor judgment.

But I'm not dead. I'm alive and I itch. There's me walking over to the copy machine at work. Every step a prickly reminder of my unattractive secret. There's me standing in line for the bank machine, got my card ready, surreptitiously performing the credit card test and flunking it. Scratching away like it was a lottery ticket or something. Coming up with nothing. Another loser with shallow pockets. Shallow pockets, thank god.

Nancy Druid

Last night the laundromat was full of dim bulbs with big personalities, but you appeared to me as some sort of teenage sleuth. With good breeding, a can-do attitude, a white starched shirt with a Peter Pan collar, yet a puzzling New Age philosophy, so I referred to you as Nancy Druid.

I joined the cult of your personality for a 20% discount even though, like my mother, I'm usually not a joiner.

You had me trail you to a bar. By the way, everyone there cast their eyes slowly up, quickly down, then readjusted their seating positions and pretended they never saw you, so I figured you must be somebody famous. The bar, which had no sign, did have a name, but nobody knew it. It was owned by a comedian formerly working on an ensemble-cast late night sketch comedy show who went on to make good money for bad movies co-starring the likes of Kelsey Grammer. Give the place a living room feel, he told the design team. It's the latest. Why be home in your living room, he bellowed, when you be could out, feeling at home in a bar that just looks like your living room? It worked on me. I immediately scanned the sofa cushions for old *TV Guide*s and coins with little numismatic value.

There was a woman in the corner with two turntables and a microphone. She looked suspiciously like that shiny girl with the split lip who always tries to sell me used batteries in front of the falafel shop even when I say No Thanks.

I spied a 14-year-old screenwriter bouncing up and down in the lap of a supermodel, wasted. He had just taken a meeting with David Geffen about adapting his autobiography for the big screen. The abusive father character who made him juggle naked at fondue dinner parties would have to be played by an actor who resembled a Honeybaked Ham, he said. Kurt Russell maybe. Or Beau Bridges.

My vodka rocks was made with Ketel One automatic and cost $9. It was a lot but how often did I get to mingle with interesting people in a living room atmosphere even if I did blow it by staring at one of those guys I'd been reading about with the oversized metal BBs implanted in his head so the scar tissue would form little lumps and he yelled, "What're you staring at?" but I thought I had the right.

I waited in line for the bathroom with a girl who worked behind the MAC counter at Macy's and spoke each sentence interrogatively. She said my face had potential? but it was all wrong? and that I should come in? and see her? she could fix it? When I walked into the stall after her I noticed she had peed all over the seat and left it there for me to clean up. Somehow, I didn't feel worthy so I walked out, and the woman behind me was yelling, "Nice work, you incontinent slut!" at me. Like I did it or something. Her friends pointed with grossed-out faces from junior high. I would head straight for the door as soon as I could locate it.

Later that night I told Dear Diary that visiting the living room bar was a real Stations of the Cross experience. Though initially interested in the drama unfolding, I was ultimately, all along, aware of the outcome.

Someone to Contact

I met her at the Elk's Lodge off of Highway 13. They wouldn't
let the wives come in unless it was for a special party, but they had
the two of us girls tending bar for them. They called us the Gold-
Dust Twins, which was funny because we didn't look alike at all.
We only knew each other for a couple of weeks before she left and
got the job working for that guy, Russ Talbot. I don't know whose
idea it was in the first place to hire her as a personal assistant to a
private investigator. I mean, a six-foot-tall redhead behind the wheel
of that beat-up car. Just primer. That's what she drove. Following
tax evaders and card players, cheating husbands or wives. A lot of
that kind of thing. We got together once after she left the Lodge.
We just went shopping over at the new mall and had lunch. She
seemed a lot happier, sort of sillier, more like a little kid than when

I'd first met her.

No, she didn't say much about the new job. Only that she liked the hours, working at night, because she had trouble sleeping a lot. She was an insomniac. Insomniac. That was one of the first things she told me about herself. I remember because I thought it was a little weird. Most days, I fall asleep before my head hits the pillow. Um, yeah, she liked her boss. He used to be a police officer in Bakersfield or somewhere and his brother drove one of those roach-coaches. You know one of those trucks that brings sandwiches and sodas down to the office park. With the funny horns. One of those.

I only knew that because she said one day they had her working in the roach-coach too. Keeping her eyes out for some guy, I'm not sure. I remember the part about how she said the men, the workers buying their lunches, all flirted with her. I can just picture it. She was so bubbly and it wasn't fake. That's just how she was. I can see her wearing those big sunglasses she had inside the shiny metal of one of those trucks. It's been so sunny and hot lately. I had a hard time going to work yesterday myself. It seemed like a day to play hooky and drink beer. I can see why maybe she would decide to go somewhere like that. I might do the same thing if I was in her position.

All I really know is what I read in the papers and saw on the news. A couple of the people from t.v., one that I recognized from Channel Five, the black lady, came to my apartment this morning. That's how I found out. They showed me some pictures and told me. I never knew she had put me down as someone to contact. I don't think I ever gave her my address. I wasn't even sure she knew my last name. I mean, I hardly knew her.

The Other Cheers

Do you know this place Cheapos? The cheap gas place? It's right off Highway One near Pacifica. Well, that's where I stopped to fill up on the way back home. I thought I could make it the whole way, but then the gas light came on, so I said fuck it and stopped. As I'm standing there pumping my gas, I heard what sounded like a party coming from across the street in this strip mall. It looked like maybe there was a bar down in the back corner and people were spilling out into the parking lot. I guess it was about 9 p.m.

The fog had rolled in and I was freezing, standing out there in my sarong and flip-flops. I'd been at the beach all day with my sister and her kids and it was blazing. We all got a little sunburned and besides the part where Heather freaked out on Zachary for flashing his little thingy at other kids, it was a really fun day. Since I've just gotten to the point where I can hang out with my family again, I'm trying to be really chill and open-minded about everything, even though it kept getting on my nerves how neurotic and controlling Heather and Jose are with the kids. Whatever. I get to be the crazy aunt they worship and then I get to go back to my apartment by myself where everything is just how I want it.

So I'm at Cheapos and I go up to the guy in the booth to buy a bottle of water. The first thing he says is, "Hey! Where's your green?" I thought he meant my money, or else marijuana, but first I thought he meant money, so I said, "Oh. I just paid with my card at the pump, but I have cash for the water. How much?"

"No," he says, "St. Patrick's Day. I get to pinch you if you're not wearing green." I hadn't even realized it was St. Patrick's Day. I had totally forgotten. It's not like I'm Irish or anything, well, I might be, but it just seemed sort of unsettling that I had missed a holiday. Wasn't missing holidays a thing for depressed people? Or else people who didn't pay much attention to life in general? I hadn't been either of those in years, so it was really sort of shocking. I hoped I wasn't slipping.

"I don't see any green," he says again, holding the water above his head like someone teasing a dog with one of those Snausages.

The kids didn't even mention it today. Kids are supposed to get into that sort of thing, aren't they? Holidays? I remember me and my friend covering ourselves in little green shamrocks we'd made out of construction paper and wearing buttons that said "Kiss Me, I'm Irish." Maybe it's not cool anymore. Maybe all of the littler holidays are getting overshadowed by Christmas.

The weird thing about this gas station guy was that he was actually kind of cute. Not that I have a "type" or anything, but he was probably late thirties, closer to my age than a lot of men I'd been meeting. He had a thin little moustache, kind of like Rhett

Butler or Freddie Mercury, and slicked back hair. He also wore a dangly earring, which seemed sort of cheesy, but great blue eyes. Really light blue with these thick black lashes that were all curled back and pretty. The kind of eyelashes where, at some point, a grandmother or other older female relative probably said something stupid to him, like "What a waste for God to put those on a boy."

"Well, where's *your* green?" I say back to him. "Maybe I get to pinch you." I don't know what I was thinking, flirting back like this, but it was fun. Then he said something cute, like "Wouldn't you like to know?" or "Why don't you try and find it?" and next thing I know he's out of his little cashier box saying, "You must be freezing. Where are you from?" and all that.

I tell him I'm originally from Salinas but now I live in Colma, and he says, "Hey! Me too!" I was trying to figure out if he meant he was originally from Salinas or that now he lived in Colma, or both, when he says," My name's Marty," and believe me, I don't know why, but I said, "Me too!" I was just nervous, I guess. He says, "That's a funny name for a girl," and then I remembered a friend of my mother's and I say, "It is not! Martha. It's really Martha."

He goes, "Okay, Marty. Settle down! I was just going to go on over there to Cheers and get a drink. You wanna come with?"

"It's called Cheers?" I say. "Like the t.v. show?"

"Where everybody knows your name," he says.

I couldn't believe there was another bar named Cheers. I had visited the real one once when I was in Boston and got the T-shirt. Been there. Done that. Bought the T-shirt. (I also had the T-shirt that said that.) Who knew there was one just ten miles from my house? I had to go. Plus tomorrow was my day off and what was I going to do if I went home now anyway? There was some party Ginny told me about in the Sunset, but I wasn't about to go home and shower and change just to hang out with her friends from work who'd no doubt be completely shit-faced by the time I got there.

"Okay," I say. "Let me get some clothes on."

I open up my trunk and rummage around until I find an old sweater. I'd gotten it for Christmas a few years ago from my mom. It was pretty ugly, one of those big knits with spangles and baubles making up a Christmas tree design on the front. I had used it a couple times to wipe off the dipstick when I was checking the oil, but there were only a few marks under one of the armpits. You could barely see them. Most importantly, it was green.

"That's quite a sweater you have there, Marty," Marty says.

"Oh, shut up Marty!" I say. We're getting along great already.

I start to get into my car and Marty says, "Hey! I thought we were having a drink," and I say, "Well, yeah. Aren't we going to drive? There's plenty of close spaces there in the lot." And Marty says, "Let's walk. Let's take a moonlight stroll."

I leave my car right where it's at and Marty locks up the booth. We walk out of the fluorescent spotlight of the station and onto the dark pavement of Coronet Boulevard. My forehead is wet from the fog and the air smells like ocean and smoke.

We get halfway across the street, onto the little median strip that's planted full of pink and white oleanders, when it occurs to me that I've been here before. It was the hair salon at the far end of the mall called All That Hair Jazz that tipped me off. Hair salons always had dumb names like Curl Up and Dye and The Hairport, but this name really didn't make any sense to me. You could have put any business name into that phrase. All That Coffee Jazz or All That Pool Supplies Jazz. It wasn't very clever, was it? But I'd been here, all right. We're right around the corner from this guy I used to work with, Joe Something or other. We worked together once at this big computer company and he quit right before we all got laid off. It was a big bummer for him because he didn't get any unemployment and I heard it took him forever to find another job.

There was this one day where me and Joe and a couple other

yahoos slipped out of the office early and drove here to his house near the beach. We all lived in cruddy apartments, so we were really excited about seeing this whole beach house he had. It turned out to be kind of cruddy, too. It smelled real mildewy and his furniture was all beat up. It really just made everybody like Joe all the more knowing he wasn't better off than the rest of us. Joe was having fun playing host. He kept making us Seabreezes all afternoon and then, when we ran out of liquor and got hungry, we came down to the taco place right there. Next to All That Hair Jazz.

So I say to Marty, "I've got a friend who lives around here. I should call him up and see if he wants to come over and celebrate."

"Maybe he's already there," he says. "It sounds like just about the whole town's there."

Joe probably was down at his local bar on St. Patrick's Day. He had a bit of a drinking problem, but he was such a laugh riot when he drank, nobody minded. He did impersonations like nobody's business. Lots of movie stars and not only the last ten presidents, but the last ten vice presidents as well. You wouldn't think somebody could do Walter Mondale, but Joe was that good. Linda, who was also in our department, sent me an email a few months ago saying Joe and his wife had had a baby. Nobody from work had ever met his wife, she was from somewhere near Russia, but Linda said the whole family was doing fine and the kid was fat and happy.

We get up toward Cheers and people are spilling out into the parking lot, smoking, and there's a couple of big motorcycle guys in their leathers sitting on their bikes out front. Some of the women are dressed real skimpy, but I guess I'm wearing a sarong and a bathing suit. At least I was covered up with the Christmas sweater.

Marty seemed to know a lot of people which made me feel safer. Not that I was feeling all that weird, but you know. You go to a strange bar with a man and who knows what could happen? Well, actually I know exactly what could happen. I had a lot of wild times when I was in my twenties, before I got my shit together, and I didn't want to repeat any of that again.

The minute we walk in the door someone hands us a couple of green beers and we each pick up a pair of green plastic leprechaun ears from a big bucket on the bar. Marty starts introducing me around right off saying, "This fine lady's name is Marty," and I was joking, "Oh, yeah. He just picked me up at the gas station," and everyone laughed.

The band they got is really smoking. I think they're called Party Over Here or maybe it's Party Over There, but anyway they do a real range of music from '50s stuff to hard rock and some songs I recognize from the whole disco era. I had been staying out of bars for years now and it was amazing to see the whole scene was just the same as it used to be.

The beers start going to my head a little, but I was feeling great. At one point, Marty pulls me by my ears out on the dance floor and we get into these wild dance moves, acting like chickens or something, with everyone standing around us laughing. I take a little breather and get the urge to look up Joe in the phone book. Joe Something Long and Italian with a B. I plop myself down on the floor and start going through the book. Baciagaluppi. There it was. Can you believe it? I go running to Marty to see if he has any change and he's busy flirting with the bartender, not that I cared really, everyone was being free and easy that night. I say, "Baciagaluppi. That's my friend Joe I was talking about. I found his number in the book." And Marty says, "That's who you're talking about? Big Joe B.? He's the greatest! From the carpet place!"

"I'm going to call him. Do you have change?"

The bartender picks up the phone and dials the number from memory and hands me the receiver, "Here you go, Marty."

There's really a racket in the there, but I hear a man's voice pick up and I yell, "Joe! Joe! It's Tina! From the Key Microsystems days!"

I see Marty and the bartender look at each other.

"Listen, I'm at Cheers! Down the street from you. Come have a drink! I can't hear you! Come over!"

I hand the phone back to Deb and she says, "Hey, I thought you said your name was Marty." I get all embarrassed and Marty looks at me and says, "Marty. Tina. Let's get you another beer."

Marty buys me a drink and tells me he's known Joe for a couple years now. I guess Joe's been having some problems with his wife and now they've got that baby on top of it. He hasn't been at the bar so much now that they've got the kid, but he hosted a poker night for the boys a few months back. Marty said Joe's Russian wife stayed in the bedroom the whole time and when he was looking for the bathroom, he accidentally opened the wrong door and she was in there wearing nothing but her bra and a slip and laying on the bed staring straight up at the ceiling. She didn't even look over at him when he opened the door.

It seems like right when Marty says he doesn't expect Joe will show up, there he is walking in the door. Like a cue on a t.v. show. A little chunkier, but smiling from ear to ear. I run up and give him a big hug, which is probably odd considering I've never hugged him before, but who cares. It was St. Patty's Day.

Joe starts right in with the impressions and everybody gathers around him shouting out requests. "Do Jimmy Carter!" somebody's yelling. "Do Tricky Dick!"

About here is where it all starts getting a little hazy. I remember dancing some more and one of the guys from the band pulling me up on stage to play tambourine. Then Joe came over and lifted me off the stage and started spinning me around on the dance floor really fast until I was yelling at him to stop because I was getting sick. My sarong flew off and I remember these guys playing "keep away" with it until Marty punched one of them.

I guess the fight broke out then, but I wasn't paying much attention because all of a sudden a lady wearing an overcoat over her pajamas shows up. She's yelling at Joe in Russian, I think. Or maybe her accent was so thick that it just sounded like it wasn't English. You know how that happens with foreigners sometimes? Well, all I could think of was the baby. That baby everyone had been talking about. Where was the baby? All these drunk people and nobody's watching the baby.

Some guy tried to grab me as I ran out of the bar. I think it was Marty. I didn't care about him and his stupid friends anymore. I needed to rescue the baby from these terrible people. We could go out to the beach where the air was clean. The fresh air would do us some good. Now if I could just remember how to get to their house I could grab the baby. What a shame. All alone on a holiday.

Back To The Future

The invitation said "casual evening wear" so I selected a beautiful floral Gunne Sax by Jessica McClintock that was floor length and had an extremely tight-fitting bodice that accentuated the 32 A-ness of my breasts. I also purchased a wig of cascading red curls and a large pair of drugstore bifocals with a kicky lavender tint. When I got ready to go, the look achieved turned out to be remarkably like a mysterious cousin of Howard Stern's doing a stint on *Little House On The Prairie*. Or else Barbra Streisand if she never got famous and instead was the wife of a furniture showroom dealer who raced ATVs on the weekends. I was looking good and ready for action.

More and more in these busy times, high school reunions are organized by professional reunion organizing businesses with catchy names. The Prospect High Class of '90 reunion was put on by a company called Back To The Future Reunions and they had it all figured out. Upon arrival, everyone got a nice round photo button with their senior portrait on it and for an extra three dollars you could buy a shot glass emblazoned with a purple panther. If you wanted the works, there was a booklet available for five dollars that explained what everyone had been up to since graduation. All I remember about my own entry is that I was sort of drunk when I filled it out and it began with the phrase, "After the intervention...."

My friend Amy's dad offered to drop us off at the sterile convention center locale because he didn't want us drinking and driving. I'm not sure what he thought we were doing the other 364 days of the year, but it was an offer we couldn't refuse. He assured us that we should call him when we wanted to be picked up, no matter what time it was. I'm sure some of our former classmates wouldn't have touched this offer with their twelve-foot polevaulting poles, but I had different hang-ups. Like not being able to attend my ten-year reunion as myself.

As soon as Mr. Nicholas dropped us off, Amy and I pretended not to know one another. We've been friends since second grade and we knew if she were seen palling around with a freak, people would figure it out quick. I whispered my name to the woman working the door and she eyed me with pity and handed over the photo button. I quickly put it in my crocheted clutch and took a look around. No one else was wearing their photo buttons either. Someone, perhaps drill team captain Donna Corkindale or downhill ski champ Jason Byrne, had already made that decision for everyone. Just because the photo button has a pin and is meant to be pierced through clothing and worn, you are not supposed to actually wear it.

Apparently, what you were supposed to wear was a sarcastic black cocktail dress. Nearly every other woman besides Amy in her '60s sheath was wearing a version of the same black sleeveless number with gold jewelry accessorizing their well-exercised necks and wrists. You know all those stories where people say, "So-and-so got really fat," and "So-and-so is divorced and miserable." Everyone at my reunion just looked like they worked out a lot.

I began the evening as I planned, rocking back and forth in the corner on my heels and slurping loudly from my plastic cup. A pack of well-groomed young ladies began to point and laugh. I never wanted it to end.

The disc jockey team was from Fremont. They played "Come On, Eileen" and I was the first to hit the dance floor. Everyone was trying very hard not to overtly make fun of the spasmodic mysterious cousin of Howard Stern who was me, but Amy nearly blew my cover when she almost peed in her pants laughing.

Another time-honored tradition at high school reunions seems to be finding out who is gay. Half of my friends now are queer and, as it turned out, half of my friends have always been queer. When good old gay Peter Rosen, insightfully deducing my get-up as a costume, came up and looked into my eyes, he grabbed me by the hand saying, "Oh my god! From now on, you are my date!" He paraded me about the parquet and its industrial-carpeted shores as speculation mounted: Man in drag or pathetic attempt at "beard"?

Finally, after three hours in the outfit, the jig was up. Word had spread about my real identity and I commend myself for recognizing it was time to toss in the Gunne Sax. I went into the bathroom to change and was relieved to discover the cheerleaders and the stoners had finally settled their differences over shared Marlboro Lights.

"Casey Pollack, you're crazy!" they all said. "I can't believe you made yourself look so ugly!' I modestly pulled off my wig and there was an audible gasp at my sweaty, matted-down hair, which, due to a dying mishap, was the color of urine after too many vitamins. I stripped right there in front of them, not even bothering to go into a stall, and put on a slip I had crumpled up in my backpack.

The strap ripped as I was pulling it on and while Tamara Kravitz repeated the same bit of rote dialogue I'd overheard her say to at least ten other people that evening: *I live in Redondo, I'm a dietician and I'm engaged!*

I tucked the broken strap under my hairy armpit and emerged back on the dance floor in my lingerie toga looking as silly as everyone else, just in a different way. As Amy and I boogied down to the hits of the '80s, I started to wonder why I decided to do this in the first place. I used to be sensitive. I used to cry when I saw that toothless old lady with the pet squirrel playing the musical saw on the park bench. I used to wonder if the retarded guy eating the smashed sandwich at the bus stop had anyone who loved him. Now I've reduced myself to mocking everyone I went to high school with.

"You think you look good?" I seemed to be saying. "You think you were going to come back here and impress everyone?" I seemed to be implying via my messy presentation and dirty toenails. "Well, look at me! I look like shit!" Exactly what was the point again?

As if she could sense my momentary fragility, Patty Spalding walked straight up to me and said, "Casey Pollack. You were so mean to me at Congress Springs Elementary. In the fourth grade. You made my life miserable!"

I felt terrible. Kids are so awful. I almost buckle under and apologize, but then I remember. I already apologized to her for this when she brought it up in ninth grade algebra. We sat next to each other all semester and everything seemed fine after that. What was her problem?

"And you have lipstick on your teeth," she says.

I tower over her in my dumb shoes and remember the fateful line from the playground as if someone was presenting it to me on a cue card.

"Hamburger Butt Patty," I scowl. "Jethro Tull is a band. Not just one guy."

Beth Lisick is a writer and performer. She is the author of *Monkey Girl* (Manic D Press) and fronts a band, The Beth Lisick Ordeal. She has performed at National Poetry Slams, South by Southwest Music Festivals, and numerous writing conferences. She has been the opening act for Exene Cervenka, Lydia Lunch, Neil Young, and the late Allen Ginsberg. Lisick has toured the U.S. alone, with the spoken word group Sister Spit, and has also performed her work throughout Western Europe. Her writing has appeared in *Best American Poetry* (Scribner), *Slam!* (Penguin), *Sex and Single Girls* (Seal), and *American Poetry: The Next Generation* (Carnegie-Mellon University), among other publications. She is a columnist at SFGate.com, and recently portrayed a cop in a new music video by Sparklehorse. Lisick resides in Berkeley, California.

Manic D Press Books

Harmless Medicine. Justin Chin. $13.95
Depending on the Light. Thea Hillman. $13.95
Escape from Houdini Mountain. Pleasant Gehman. $13.95
Poetry Slam: the competitive art of performance poetry. Gary Glazner, ed. $15
I Married An Earthling. Alvin Orloff. $13.95
Cottonmouth Kisses. Clint Catalyst. $12.95
Fear of A Black Marker. Keith Knight. $11.95
Red Wine Moan. Jeri Cain Rossi. $11.95
Dirty Money and other stories. Ayn Imperato. $11.95
Sorry We're Close. J. Tarin Towers. $11.95
Po Man's Child: a novel. Marci Blackman. $12.95
The Underground Guide to Los Angeles. Pleasant Gehman, ed. $13.95
The Underground Guide to San Francisco. Jennifer Joseph, ed. $14.95
Flashbacks and Premonitions. Jon Longhi. $11.95
The Forgiveness Parade. Jeffrey McDaniel. $11.95
The Sofa Surfing Handbook. Juliette Torrez, ed. $11.95
Abolishing Christianity and other short pieces. Jonathan Swift. $11.95
Growing Up Free In America. Bruce Jackson. $11.95
Devil Babe's Big Book of Fun! Isabel Samaras. $11.95
Dances With Sheep. Keith Knight. $11.95
Monkey Girl. Beth Lisick. $11.95
Bite Hard. Justin Chin. $11.95
Next Stop: Troubletown. Lloyd Dangle. $10.95
The Hashish Man and other stories. Lord Dunsany. $11.95
Forty Ouncer. Kurt Zapata. $11.95
The Unsinkable Bambi Lake. Bambi Lake with Alvin Orloff. $11.95
Hell Soup: the collected writings of Sparrow 13 LaughingWand. $8.95
Revival: spoken word from Lollapalooza 94. Torrez, et al.,eds. $12.95
The Ghastly Ones & Other Fiendish Frolics. Richard Sala. $9.95
King of the Roadkills. Bucky Sinister. $9.95
Alibi School. Jeffrey McDaniel. $11.95
Signs of Life: channel-surfing through '90s culture. Joseph, ed. $12.95
Beyond Definition. Blackman & Healey, eds. $10.95
Love Like Rage. Wendy-o Matik. $7
The Language of Birds. Kimi Sugioka. $7
The Rise and Fall of Third Leg. Jon Longhi. $9.95
Specimen Tank. Buzz Callaway. $10.95
The Verdict Is In. edited by Kathi Georges & Jennifer Joseph. $9.95
Elegy for the Old Stud. David West. $7
The Back of a Spoon. Jack Hirschman. $7
Baroque Outhouse/Decapitated Head of a Dog. Randolph Nae. $7
Graveyard Golf and other stories. Vampyre Mike Kassel. $7.95
Bricks and Anchors. Jon Longhi. $8
Greatest Hits. edited by Jennifer Joseph. $7
Lizards Again. David Jewell. $7
The Future Isn't What It Used To Be. Jennifer Joseph. $7

Please add $4 to all orders for postage and handling.
Manic D Press • Box 410804 • San Francisco CA 94141 USA
info@manicdpress.com   www.manicdpress.com
Trade Distribution: US & Canada by Publishers Group West
                           UK & Europe by Turnaround Distribution